HIS HALLOWEEN SWEET

A MALE/MALE HALLOWEEN ROMANCE

RAVEN DE HART

For my father, the only person I've ever known to have a literal bar filled with candy when you walk into the house.

FIND RAVEN DE HART ONLINE

Connect with Raven de Hart
Newsletter
Facebook
Twitter
Instagram
Website

Read Other Books from Raven de Hart
Priorities Trilogy
The Christmas Interlude
Write Time for a Second Chance
Swarm
Silverfall
Heart of a Pirate

CHAPTER ONE

*L*achlan James's nose tingled with the effervescence of pasilla and lime zest as the oils exploded in the warm sugar. He was trying a new brittle, though he wasn't sure how well it was going to work. Pumpkin seeds, chili, and citrus in the starkly sweet candy. The nose, at least at this early stage, was promising, though he couldn't say for certain it would appeal all that much to the palates of his general clientele.

Well, who he hoped would be his general clientele. At the moment, James and Co. Candy Shop was less the hub of Cape Elizabeth and more a not-quite self-sustaining relic of better days. He'd inherited it from his father, who left to go live out his retirement in the Caribbean and only checked in to criticize and complain about Lachlan's life. His father had inherited it from his own mother, who was a sweet enough woman, but at ninety-nine, wasn't going out and getting involved in the business very much anymore.

Honestly, the only thing that kept Lachlan from having to live in the actual shop was the side-business he'd also inherited. The James family went *back* in Maine, all the way to 1820, and for the majority of that time, they were one of the premier magical families working in all of the New England area. The candy making was a nice hobby, passed through the family along with the spell codices, that created a convenient cover for them to set up shop and work their witchcraft for those who needed it and knew what they could provide.

Both were honest work, but only one of the two had ever carried the risk of being tarred and feathered and hanged from the boughs of a pine tree. So the magic stayed hidden.

He pushed the brittle aside to cool and sighed, glancing around the workspace. Some old, inherited candy machines filled the kitchen, along with cases of various molds and rollers to form the sugar for the more complex candies. Not brittle, of course. But little lozenges, candies shaped like various fruits and flowers, and the classic triangular humbug shape. All of those took a little more than just pouring molten sugar into a pan.

He glanced at the calendar hanging above the sink. The 24th of October. *Maybe I should take it down.* His stomach tightened and slipped down into his feet every time he looked at it lately, at his hopeful red circle around the Halloween. If ever a candy shop should have been able to slip into the black, it was in the lead-up to Halloween. Especially his pretentious— he fully admitted his shop was pretentious in at least half a dozen different ways—candy store in Cape Elizabeth. Plenty of rich folks who should have wanted something a little fancier than the mass-produced candy bars and bulk bags that currently filled the grocery store shelves. Yet here he stood, trying experimental candies alone in his kitchen, and considering whether it was moral to turn some magic onto his own finances to float him for a few months so he wouldn't lose the family legacy.

He'd decided against it, but only because he'd gotten an email, asking for him to work up a spell to keep a local woman's husband faithful. Any spell that took animal sacrifice, he always upcharged because…animal sacrifice. The fish had been zero cost, since he caught it himself that morning, but he'd still had to slaughter and butcher it.

So...upcharge.

The bell above the front door tinkled, and Lachlan headed out front. He got the odd lookie-loo, so he didn't expect a whole lot more than that. Still, he could attempt to pressure someone into buying. So he swept through the stainless steel door and out into the shop proper. The scent of chili and lime was left behind, replaced with a cacophony of fruits and spices from the various jars of candy strewn about the shop. Jars filled with little sugary jewels in every color of the rainbow, and a dozen more that had no place in any rainbow anywhere. He ducked his head around one of the paper bats he'd hung from the ceiling and put on his best customer service smile.

And he nearly lost it when he saw the customer who'd come in. Slight of build, probably about five-five. Black hair, but with brassy highlights dyed in along the underside. Some sort of Asian descent. Korean, perhaps Japanese? He didn't know. But strikingly fine-boned, pale peachy skin, cheeks flushed rosy from the autumn chill. He wore a black sweater with a starkly Missoni-esque pattern on it, but chunkier and bolder. Green and red and yellow zigzags slicing across his chest and adorning the cuffs.

So it took Lachlan a few seconds before he finally spoke up. "Let me know if you need help with anything."

The gentleman nodded, then headed straight for the front desk. He pushed his thin-framed circular glasses back up his nose as he approached. "I'm actually hoping I can get a sample of some of this?"

"Samples, yeah." Lachlan knew it was the best way to run the shop, let people taste the product, but especially when money got at its tightest, he hated it. A lot of folks just came in and "sampled" his candy, then left with a wave and all their money still in their wallets. But he nodded and rummaged through some of what he had behind the counter. "I've got a few things back here I made this morning." He filled a tiny sample cup with a few pieces of candy. "The pink one is watermelon, and the gummies are some old school flavors. Green for clove, white for mint, and red for cinnamon."

The stranger took the clove gummy and popped it back, chewing silently before swallowing. "That is *intense*." He half-chuckled. "Good thing I like clove." He smiled, bright white and straight and even, and Lachlan felt a sudden, unwelcome flush attempting to creep up his chest, his neck, into his ears.

So much so he swept back and out of the room. "I have some fresh pumpkin seed brittle, too." He checked it and, at least on the edge, it had set enough he could crack something off. Why he'd gone with *that* as his excuse, he didn't know. Just flustered by suddenly being so attracted to this random customer. *Like hot people never show up here or something.* But now he was committed, so he had to bring something back. He cracked a corner off with the back of a spoon and carried it out. "There's some pasilla chilis in here, so if you can't handle heat, maybe not the best."

"I'm Korean," he said by way of excuse, then took the brittle and crunched into it. Lachlan hadn't actually *tested* the brittle yet, so he waited, watching for any sign. When the new guy hadn't said anything for what was definitely at least a decade, Lachlan opened his mouth to explain, but was interrupted. "That's much more what I'm looking for." Another slight laugh passed over the guy's lips. "I'll take...I don't know how this works, do I order by the pound?"

"It's by weight, yeah. I just have the one batch, though, and it needs to finish setting."

"Well I can wait." He sighed. "Do you do big batch orders, too?"

Okay, I guess he's not in here just to steal all my samples. Which presented the slight problem of him needing to close down the shop and sell a two-hundred-seventy-five dollar mackerel dinner to this random woman in the next twenty minutes. "I take orders, yeah."

"Awesome. My family's got a big Halloween party coming up, and they put me in charge of candy this year. I'd like to support a local business if I can."

Lachlan, again, was taken aback and had to pause for a few seconds before his mouth would actually make words again. "How big an order are we talking about?"

"Well, we have the party, the trick-or-treaters, my family's sweet tooth, my own sweet tooth…" He smiled demurely and pushed his glasses up one more time. "We normally budget a few hundred dollars for the candy, but if that's not enough, I'm sure we could negotiate higher."

"A few hundred?" Lachlan didn't catch himself before spouting off. "Sorry. I don't mean to offend."

"I'm not offended. It's objectively a lot of money. But it's a big party, and if you don't let yourself gorge on candy during a Halloween party, when are you going to let yourself at all?"

Finally, someone gets it. He sampled his own wares more often than he was entirely comfortable admitting, and he always made sure he had extra when trick-or-treaters were incoming, because with that much candy around, he knew he was going to eat a ton of it. Lachlan glanced to the clock and saw that he was running short. "Look, I have a client coming in soon, but I can definitely tackle your order for you. Just leave your name and number, and we can set up a time for you to come in, discuss what it is you're going to need?" He pulled out his little-used appointment pad, doing his best to wipe the thing veneer of dust off without being too obvious, and slipped it across.

The guy took it. "I'll see you…hopefully tomorrow?" He finished scratching down his information—Colby was his name, and he'd included two phone numbers and an email address—then sighed. "I know you said the brittle wasn't ready, but is there any way I can go home with some?"

As long as you go home. The fidelity spell he had in the works was more than just an expensive fish. Saltpeter, underwear from the couple burned in a ritual fire, and lemon for flavor. He mostly didn't want to try and answer questions about the underwear burning, though, and he *really* didn't want to scare this client away. "I can probably part with four ounces, but it might stick together as it cools."

"That's fine."

He nodded and slid into the back, quickly breaking up part of the pan into manageable shards. He brought those out on a cute little quarter sheet pan. "Since it's a recipe I'm still working on, we'll call it eight bucks."

"You'll take twenty."

Your money, Colby boy. Lachlan wrapped the pieces up in parchment, then tucked the parcel into a little forest green box emblazoned with "James and Co." across the lid. "Here's this, and I'll call you as soon as I can."

Colby passed the twenty across and took his box of brittle. "Thanks. I'll leave you to your work. And it's good brittle, by the way. If you're still wondering about the recipe."

"Good can always be better."

Colby smiled as he turned away, and the bells signaled him leaving. Which meant Lachlan could head back…and since the brittle was already on his mind, he could give it a taste. He snapped off a one-inch section and popped it into his mouth. The sugar was good, hard and crackable. As he let it dissolve, he got the lime first. Not super intense. *Could stand a little bit of flavoring oil.* And as he chewed, a mild warmth and smokiness moved through his mouth. The pasilla, at least, was nicely balanced. Not too hot, but present. What it desperately needed was salt to offset not only the acidic lime, but the fat content of the pumpkin seeds. But all in all…good. Good was the proper descriptor.

He waited ten minutes for the appointment, and even gave her another fifteen on top of that. Then he emailed, and got a mailer daemon back. Apparently she'd used a burner email. So that money was off the table, and he had to have mackerel for dinner. *Will the horrors never cease?*

So while he cooked the mackerel up in a hot skillet—sans saltpeter, since *he* wasn't cheating on anyone. That would have required him to actually be in a relationship to begin with, and not just with his own insecurities—he rolled this new order around in his head. A few hundred dollars worth of candy, all to be ready in time for Halloween, and all he knew about his new client was his name, his contact info, and that he liked clove and the weird pumpkin seed brittle. Which, to be fair, Lachlan also enjoyed enough that he'd taken the samples home with him. He'd been right about the salt, too. It definitely benefited from a good sprinkling of rock salt. He'd used that pretentious, pink Himalayan salt that he'd bought a year ago, because what the hell else was he going to use it for if not this?

The clock ticked past six thirty by the time the fish, the asparagus, and the rice were finished and on his plate. He intended to finish the whole fish, because you didn't make a ritual sacrifice out of an animal, then not eat the entire thing. That was just plain disrespectful, and a good way to get the spirits of nature in a shit mood with you to boot. For fish, it wasn't bad at all. But Lachlan really didn't care for fish. With liberal application of some wine, he managed to choke the whole lot of it down. That still only put it at seven, and his whole body still vibrated from everything that had gone down today.

Mostly, it vibrated with the thought of Colby. Maybe more specifically, the look of him, and the gentle, careful voice that parted his lips when he spoke, and the way his cheeks had been pink from the autumnal air. Even his glasses had played into the delicate features, the slim build. His dark eyes had been unfairly captivating, pools of ink that demanded to be seen.

When Lachlan had packed up the leftover rice and drained the last bit of wine from the bottle, it was still far too early to try and turn in, and the thought of trying to sit down and watch TV or read a book, something that inactive, it just made his skin crawl. He felt the need to be doing, to be fighting for this business, even though he had no real way of being able to fight for it right now.

Well, one way. He scurried over to his computer, opened his email, and shot off a quick missive to Colby.

Hey, Colby.

I'm just checking in before I forget. I'll still call tomorrow to setup a proper appointment, but if you're the kind of person who would rather write your thoughts out, I thought an email would be better-suited to that sort of thing. Dealer's choice.

Talk to you soon,
Lachlan James,
James and Co. Candy Company

He wasn't expecting anything from that email, of course. Not really. It had been entirely to assuage his worries, not to actually get any work done. But worrying over an email would at least *feel* like work. So the second time he checked back into his inbox, the waiting reply was a shock. A welcome shock, but a shock nonetheless.

I'm free now if you want to talk. Not to impose, but if you don't want to have to wait until the morning.

C

Lachlan didn't hesitate long before pulling out his phone. The only reason he waited at all was so he didn't scare off his one somewhat significant client before he even officially started the job or got paid for it or anything. But inside three minutes, he had himself set up at the kitchen table, notepad at the ready, phone ringing on speaker.

"Hello?"

"Hi, Colby. This is Lachlan from James and Co."

"I figured it might be."

"Right. I hope I wasn't pressuring you. This can wait."

"Pressuring me to talk about delicious candy? Right, I'm in *such* a terrible position." There came that slight half-chuckle again. "I can really come in any time tomorrow. I'm home from college, so my days are pretty open. Plus I get up at the crack of dawn."

"Well, I won't make you meet up with me at the crack of dawn." Lachlan laughed at his own joke, then bit that laughter off because *wow*, talk about cringe. *Behave like a normal human being, damn it.* "How does nine o'clock work for you? The shop's usually pretty dead that early in the morning." Which wasn't inaccurate. The shop just happened to also be pretty dead at all the rest of the times, too.

"Nine is perfect. I can bring coffee if you need."

"You're the client. It's my job to take care of what you need."

"What if what I needed was to buy you a latte on the way to our meeting? Because frankly, if your brittle prices are anything to go by, you're vastly undercharging, so it's the least I can do."

"I mean, I can't stop you." Lachlan was *so* glad this was happening over the phone, not in person, because his cheeks currently burned, and at least the phone didn't give that away. "Anyway, I'll see you tomorrow."

"I'll be there with bells on. Oh, and by the way, the family loved that brittle."

"Well, it was all right. Needed some tweaking."

"Tweaking, sure, but it was still amazing. Please add that to the list of whatever you'll be making for the party. Just for me."

"It's all for you." What were those weird, burbling sensations moving through Lachlan's bloodstream, in his tummy? Why did this conversation feel so...different? It wasn't a client thing. He was self-aware enough to know this had to do with the instant, gut-level attraction he'd felt toward Colby. But why was this innocuous business call pulling on those threads at all?

"All right. I'm going to grab a night cap and head to bed," said Colby. "Good night, and I'll see you in the morning. With coffee. Whether you like it or not."

"See you in the morning." And Lachlan hung up. He hadn't even jotted down the time in his notebook, but he did scribble out "pumpkin seed chili brittle," so that was something resembling work.

Now all he had to do was convince himself to calm down enough to sleep, and if he was extra lucky, stop focusing so hard on whatever this conversation was doing. *Too bad I already finished the wine.*

CHAPTER TWO

*L*achlan came in about five every morning. It helped that the shop was withing biking distance of his house. He only really had to pull his car out when he needed supplies, or was heading to a fair or something. Fairs, farmers markets, conventions? He made good money at those. Better than he made at the shop. If he thought he could have gotten away with it, he would have dropped the shop altogether, but he needed the space, the materials, and the equipment for making the candy, and his little home kitchen wouldn't do. Plus the remote sales thing wasn't quite enough to cover his costs all by itself. He was in a precarious position where the shop was struggling to stay afloat, but he also couldn't quite afford to cut it loose.

And honestly, I don't want to have to hear what Dad would say about it if I let the whole thing go. The shop was a legacy, and it was one Lachlan didn't particularly *want* to let go.

He started up the big pots, to get them heated through, and laid out his needs for the day. He wanted to keep it light so that he could devote as much time as necessary to Colby's order, but he did have two online orders he needed to fulfill, and while he had most of the candy for those already made, one of the two also wanted two pounds of his green apple lollipops. Why anyone would need two pounds of them, he couldn't say. *Not my place to question it when people give me money, anyway.*

He also knew he'd be making another batch of the pumpkin seed brittle, and got the seeds into the oven to roast off right away, so they'd have time to cool. Once all *that* was done, he headed out and just tidied the storefront a little bit. Of course, it was then he realized he didn't have a great place set up to meet with candy clients, and his stomach clenched a little bit. *This is why we come in early.* He had a nice room in the back for magic clients, but talking candy amongst the various jars of graveyard dirt and beetle carapaces was *maybe* not the best business move. Certainly not the most *appetizing* business move.

He stepped out into the dimly lit, multicolor front of the candy shop. Still decorated for Halloween, replete with bats and pumpkins and spiders in various shades of construction paper. He had a large number of shelving units and cupboards built in, some of which had been there since the founding of the shop all those decades prior, but he'd filled in the center of the room with a number of tables, each draped in forest green material to match the logo-emblazoned candy boxes.

No one was around, and this particular part of the thoroughfare wasn't lit very well by the street lamps, so he tapped into some of the magic. There wasn't *much* theatrical magic that could be done. For the most part, it was all slow acting, fields of influence, rituals, and tiny, butterfly effect adjustments. But *some* things could be handled with a flick of the wrist. Lighting a candle between the fingertips. Dusting a room with a little breath out. Finding a touch of extra space where *perhaps* there shouldn't be any remaining.

Now, he needed the space and the dusting. He had a dozen candy jars that had to fit *somewhere* without the whole store looking like a cluttered mess. That was a little trickier, especially in a space so well-defined as this one, but he focused on some of the less-visited corners and inlets of the shop's front room, let his eyes slide out of focus *just* a touch, and lo and behold, that corner there behind the taffy jars had a little extra space, enough to fit his butterscotch rounds. On the shelves above the bins of fruit gummies, two spots were open that otherwise wouldn't have been.

Within twenty minutes, Lachlan got his table cleared off, and he got his pumpkin seeds out. A little char on some of them, but honestly, that wasn't entirely unwelcome, given how sweet the brittle was. The rest of the setup was simple enough. He slid the table a bit away from the other displays, then took a breath. He drew a quick circle with the tip of his tongue against the roof of his mouth. When he released his breath, the smell of dust hit his nose, and tiny clouds of pale powder rose from every surface…and never settled. The dust was simply gone.

Witchy tricks were good.

Throughout the rest of the morning, Lachlan managed to get a new batch of brittle together, making sure to finish it with a good dose of flaky salt across the top. He'd also added some red colorant to the sugar to make it a little bit more striking, and in general, he was happy with the new product as it sat. Now, as he smacked the large lollipop molds against the table, loosing bright green candy circles into the mix of malic acid and coarse sugar, he sighed. There were worse ways his day could have gone, worse outcomes for the week leading into Halloween. *Sometimes you just need one little break for some breathing room.*

Colby had provided that little break for him.

Lachlan weighed out as close to two pounds as he could get, then added a few more to account for the weight of the sticks. The last thing he wanted to do was be stingy, get a reputation for trying to penny pinch the clients that *almost* kept him afloat.

Everything packed up properly to mitigate the hygroscopic properties of the sugar, labels printed, he ran the boxes to the post office and paid the shipping, then headed back and opened up the store. It was close enough to eight o'clock now.

To his immense shock, a familiar face walked in not long after he'd gotten the sign flipped over. Marissa Talbot, the woman who was *supposed* to eat the mackerel he'd choked down the night before.

Lachlan slapped on his most practiced customer service smile. "Mrs. Talbot. Can I help you?"

"The…with my husband?"

"Your appointment was yesterday, and I don't have the supplies for that particular bit of action today. I told you very specifically, we had to be sure of the date."

She shuffled a little in place. "I…my husband was so *present* last night, I thought maybe we'd moved past it, but then he said he was staying late at work tonight and—"

"I feel for you, I do. But I can't change the nature of things. I don't have time today to go catch another fish, kill it properly, any of that." Not to mention, if he was staying late, she wouldn't be getting him to eat the damn thing anyway, so what was really the point? "I can throw *something* together, but it's not going to be as reliable." He shuffled through his mind. Infidelity spells were a large oeuvre of magic, and he had one in particular in mind. "Did you bring the underwear with you?"

She nodded and began to dig into her bag, but Lachlan held up his hand to halt *that* nonsense. "We're in my place of business. A candy shop. Food. Come in the back and we'll do something with it."

"Thank you." Her shoulders relaxed and the tiniest, most

nervous smile passed across her thin, pink-stained lips. "I'm sorry about yesterday."

"It is what it is." At least he'd be able to salvage *some* money out of this situation. He swept her through the kitchen and back into the little witchy room off the kitchen. Dark, hung with thick fabric that disguised the otherwise quite dull, gray brick walls. The shelves were lined with all sorts of jars, filled with all manner of powders, stones, insects, the works. A tiny brazier sat in the center of the round table. Lachlan reached out and pinched his fingers together over a bit of tinder sitting in the bottom. After a few seconds, flames flared to life, crackling against the metal. "All right, sit down."

She did so quickly, and then pulled out a pair of pale blue panties, and some plaid boxers that had definitely seen better days, if the rip in the crotch was anything to go by. "Thank you for doing this."

"You don't need to thank me, just pay me." He gingerly took the boxers. "You can keep your underwear for this one. Does your husband wear these regularly?"

She nodded. "I tried to get him to throw them out, but he's stubborn."

"Perfect." He placed the boxers into the fire, and the flimsy material took to flame almost immediately, warping and unraveling and filling the tiny room with smoke. Lachlan stood and went for the jars behind him. Common ingredients for this sort of work. "Cinnamon for passion. Saltpeter to keep his lust in check. Tumbleweed to keep him from wandering." Each thing went into the fire as he went, burning to ash. The cinnamon he added with flourish, causing an explosion of sparks that was harmless, but added some decent drama.

When everything had burned down to ashes and the last flame had gone out, he swept everything together and added it to a small jar. "You're going to go home and do a load of his laundry. All of his underwear for sure, and anything else you can fit in a single load. The more often he wears it, the better. Add this to the washer. He'll be madly attracted to the one he loves." Not as completely and utterly devoted as he would have been had she fed him the fish, but it would be an improvement. "It's going to be a hundred dollars for that."

"Please. Take the whole amount." She fished into her purse and came back with a pile of twenties. "Everything I would have given you yesterday."

"Just a hundred." In this as well as the candy shop, he wasn't interested in milking people for undeserved cash. Not to mention, when you brought magic into things, you had to be careful how you behaved, lest you invite something unpleasant into your life. The nature of this sort of magic was already questionable enough without him taking a massive pay increase for putting it together.

"Well then, at least let me buy some candy."

That, Lachlan wasn't about to argue over. "I have plenty." As he led Marissa out, he glanced at the clock. 8:16. *Plenty of time*. "What are you in the mood for?"

Once she'd gone her way with two large boxes of confections—she'd been mostly trying to get him extra money, but once she'd started tasting, she seemed to really be into the actual fact that he had some good candy, and kept wanting to sample and buy more and more—Lachlan cleaned up once again, straightened everything, and simply waited.

Colby showed up about ten till. Unlike the day before, where he'd walked in wearing striking colors and patterns that swallowed up his otherwise slight frame, today he was more form-fit, with a coffee-and-cream colored sweater that hugged close around his shoulders, and midnight blue jeans that looked so pristine Lachlan almost would have guessed they'd been starched. But who the hell starched their jeans?

He walked straight up to the counter, smiling, a cardboard coffee holder swaying gently at his side. "Morning."

"Morning." Lachlan took in a too-deep breath by mistake

and was met with a lungful of heady, citric cologne that clashed intensely with the chilly, orange-leafed autumn scene spread out on the other side of the shop windows. A good clash. Bright like a strike of lightning. "I've got your order started, as much as I could. A nice new batch of brittle."

"Oh good." Colby set the little cardboard carrier on the counter, filed with four coffee cups from Let it Be Coffee a few blocks down. "I took a guess that you'd probably be down for pumpkin spice, but then I panicked because I didn't know and also got you a drip brew. And then there's tea in case you don't actually like coffee."

"I told you, you didn't have to." Citrus and coffee mingled on his nose, and Lachlan found himself surprised that he actually enjoyed the combination. *Maybe something to try. Like in a caramel?*

"I know, but I wanted to. And I can drink whatever's left over."

Lachlan leaned down close and sniffed until he got a nose of cinnamon and clove and nutmeg, then he lifted that one out. "I won't let it go to waste. But yes, I am a basic white boy who likes pumpkin spice. How'd you know?"

"You have a very basic white boy vibe." Colby smiled, then his face fell. "That wasn't offensive, was it?"

"I said it first." *At least I'm not the only awkward one here. That's a nice change of pace.* "Come on. We can chat." He led Colby over to the table set up in the center of the shop, making sure to bring his trusty notebook alongside him. Before they even started talking, he jotted down that citrus and coffee idea. He heard someone say once that writing down ideas was a really good way to get notebooks full of bad ideas, and that the good ideas would stick around without writing them down, but Lachlan preferred not to take those sorts of chances.

Once they'd settled in, he sighed. "So, just in general,

what are we looking at? I'm assuming a big fancy to-do if you're spending this much just on candy."

"It's a pretty big deal, yeah. We do it every year. I'm surprised you haven't heard about it."

"Well, lots of people have Halloween parties every year."

Colby's cheeks turned that dusky rose color again, and he took a heavy drink from his own coffee before speaking up again. "Well, not like we do. I guess I should mention, I'm Colby Grayson."

Colby Grayson. *Grayson*. This was for the *Grayson* soiree, not just some party. *Suddenly several hundred dollars spent on candy makes a hell of a lot more sense.* "Oh."

"Yeah. I'm sorry, I don't like to mention it just willy nilly. Always feels like I'm, I don't know, trying to brag? Which I'm not."

"No, I'd rather know what I'm working with here." Graysons. The Graysons didn't actually live in Cape Elizabeth, but they had a massive house on a small bluff overlooking the Atlantic Ocean, and they'd been having their big Halloween party there as long as Lachlan could remember. Not that he knew anyone who ever got to go.

Well, that wasn't entirely true. His grandmother often brought the tale up of her one and only invitation. She'd done some undisclosed favor for the matriarch of the Grayson family three generations back, and had netted herself an invitation by way of thanks. She'd never say *exactly* what the favor was, but once, when he was fifteen, she'd had one too many PBRs and had spilled that there'd been a very sick baby. Then she got very sad, and very quiet, and switched to water.

But Lachlan had nothing beyond that, and her generic descriptions of widespread debauchery, affairs, and fine wine that she had very little interest in, but was assured over and over was quality stuff.

"So, is there a theme to work with here, or just candy in general?"

"No theme, other than just Halloween." Colby slumped forward a little bit, his shoulders dropping and his jaw unclenching as they shifted off the subject of his family. "But people like my parents, and their friends, they like to let people go wild whenever they can. It's how we ended up with four gunpowder paintings in the foyer of the house in Aspen." He cringed. "*That* was bougie as shit."

Lachlan chuckled. "Hey, relax. You're paying me, remember? I'm glad you have lots and lots of money."

Colby nodded. "Anyway, they like to see people spread their wings. So do something…shocking. Make it an experience. Like that pumpkin seed brittle. Who ever thought of that?"

"So make stuff really out there. I can certainly try." Lachlan scribbled down a few more notes, but he'd go into a big thought web later, when he could get to his white board and really spread shit out. "Do I need to be concerned about allergies?"

"Nope. At least we never have before, and nobody told me about it." He took another sip of his latte. "I don't spend all that much time here, but this is good coffee."

"Where do you live? If that's not too private."

"I was going to Berkeley. Transferring somewhere up here in the east to finish it up, though."

Lachlan bit back the thrill at that. *Somewhere in the east doesn't mean you get to eye fuck him on the reg. East could very well mean New York City, where you would go if you were a finance major.* "That sounds…exciting."

"It's boring, but I love it. Plus I don't want to be one of those idiot rich kids who coasts on his parents' money forever." He took his glasses off and polished them on his sweater. "Sorry. *That* was a little much beyond the brief. I just don't want you to get the wrong idea about me." He slipped the glasses back on and fixed those dark, deep eyes straight on Lachlan. "People find out that I'm a Grayson, and they make a lot of assumptions, so I tend to get a little defensive about being...myself."

Yeah, I don't exactly want people judging me based on my folks either. Well, my dad anyway. Still, it was a telling moment, and an unexpected intimacy that...it didn't smack Lachlan in the face, couldn't have possibly been so violent. But a force. Inexorable. Pushing forward from the set of Colby's jaw, the perfected shine and style of his hair, the well-fitted strictures he wore. A shell, and his words begged Lachlan to see beneath that outward expression borrowed from his family, his college, his peer-group, and to see *him*.

And frankly, Lachlan couldn't muster much opposition to that unspoken desire. As he sat, he took a long drink of his own latte, and took in the sight of Lachlan. His nose was as slight as the rest of his figure, a tiny button in the center of his face. His lips had a distinct arch and angularity, with a deep nasal philtrum. When he swallowed, the cords of his neck bulged out against skin that ached to be touched and felt and tasted...

...and maybe that was a bit of projection on Lachlan's part. Wearing better fitting clothing and smelling so bright and wonderful and inviting didn't exactly make Colby *less* attractive than the day he'd first walked into the shop. Didn't mean he was at all interested in *anything* back.

"Well, let me run some ideas past you, see if we can get on the same page. Feel free to say no to whatever. Just spitballing."

Colby nodded and leaned back in his chair. "All right, let's start."

CHAPTER THREE

hey talked over ideas for about an hour. Well, they actually only talked about ideas for about half an hour, but then the conversation continued to flow forward. They moved from brittle to caramel to taffy to lollipops to their favorite candy as kids—Colby was a fan of licorice, which opened up a whole new realm of flavor possibilities for Lachlan to work with—to their lives as kids to their time at school. It just made perfect sense. At least in the moment.

"So I'm well-known as 'the rich kid' in class. I'd moved past being 'the Korean one,' which was nice I guess." Colby shook his head, looking up toward the ceiling. "I used to loan money to just about every one of my friends, and I never had to get them birthday or Christmas presents because I'd just forgive them the twenty bucks or whatever it was they owed me."

"That's convenient."

"I thought so. But anyway, it wasn't a huge town. My mom wanted me to go to public school to keep me humble. So it's not like it was a private school full of other rich kids. I was a big sore thumb. So one day, I got fed up and said 'screw it.' I got a rumor going about me finally making an appearance at a school dance. This was not the busiest, most exciting town, so that was *actually* something worth gossiping about. Anyway, I go all out. As much as you can at seventeen. I convince Mom that I'm capable of taking the Porsche out for the dance, I get all tuxed up, and everyone craps themselves when I walk through the doors of the gym with Randall Davidson. Six feet tall, flaming gay, dragged out in a red-sequined dress and a blonde beehive wig."

"You're kidding."

"How else was I supposed to come out? Quietly?" He shook his head, letting his smile fade slightly. Not wholly, but to normal satisfaction levels. "And the bonus was that Randall didn't have to put up with bullshit, since he was my date. The last couple dances, he'd gone in drag and gotten harassed, gotten pushed around. But no one was willing to screw with the both of us. Which is entirely because of my family's money, not because I cut a terribly imposing figure." He gestured down his body.

"I think your figure's just fine." *Shit*. Lachlan immediately went for his latte so that he didn't have to use his mouth immediately. Never mind that the cup had been empty a while now. He could think, which would be a nice change of pace, since he definitely *hadn't* been thinking when he'd…fucking complimented Colby's body. They'd just gotten so comfortable, and things between them felt remarkably natural, and the comment had simply slipped out.

"I think your figure's also just fine." Colby leaned back, the rosiness returning to his cheeks. "It's fine to find me attractive, you know."

Lachlan set his latte down. "I just…this is a professional relationship. I don't want to cross the streams on that. And I really don't want you thinking I'm just ravenous and I found out you were gay and wanted to pounce."

"I didn't think that at all." Colby sighed and pushed his

glasses back up. A gentle smile curved up his lips. "You good at overthinking?"

"Olympic level." Lachlan rolled his shoulders back. "Sorry."

"Hey, like I said, no need to apologize. I don't go to the gym because I like sweating in public. I go to keep my glutes tight." He chuckled, shaking his head. "I know, we're keeping this very professional. I'll stop. Just don't get much chance to flirt so openly. Especially with someone actually interesting. I like math, but math and finance majors don't tend to be very fascinating conversationalists."

Before Lachlan could respond, the door swung open. Melissa Talbot, sneering and carrying what looked suspiciously like a wad of boxers in her hand. When she slammed them down on the table, Lachlan saw that was indeed what they were, but all with the crotches blown totally out. "What the hell did you give me? I wanted my husband to be faithful, not to have to go clothes shopping for him."

Double shit. Lachlan needed this part of his business out and away from his big rich candy client, stat. "Let's discuss this in the back."

"Why, don't want me rescuing another client from you?" She turned her gaze toward Colby. "Whatever you're here for, you can't trust him. All he did for me was take my money and destroy *every pair of underwear* my husband has. And guess what? He's still staying late at the office tonight. Shock of all shocks. Magic my ass."

Triple shit.

"What are you on about with magic?" Colby rose from his seat, head held high. "Do you need to get some professional help?"

"I *came* for professional help. He was supposed to make my husband stay with me."

Just all the shit. Every last turd. The fastest way to get past this whole thing was to just rip the whole entire Band-Aid off.

If he did it fast enough, maybe Colby would be so shocked that he wouldn't immediately pull out of the agreement. "You asked for my help, and then you didn't show up, so I couldn't do the spell I was going to. The one I gave you would make him only lust after his one true love." I gingerly picked up a pair of dark blue Hanes by the waistband. Still damp, so I guess she came right after washing them. "The fact *you* washing his underwear with that spell made all his crotches blow out implies that you're not his one true love at this point. Seek marriage counseling, or give me a chance to catch another fish if you're that desperate to keep a man who'd rather be with his mistress."

Melissa Talbot wore heavy rings, and they cut into Lachlan's face as she slapped him. "I'm telling everyone about this."

"Right, tell everyone my magic spell didn't work. I'll definitely be the one who comes out of that looking bad."

She fumed at him, eyes piercing, and Lachlan focused on the door. With a jerk of his head, it flung open wide, knocking the bells all over the place in a messy, cacophonous jangle.

She at least took the cue and walked out, although she left the pile of damp undies sitting in the middle of the table, between Lachlan and his client that she may very well have just lost him. *Damage control.* "So that was different."

Colby nodded and sat back down. "So magic?"

"It's a side-business. How much is going to be too much for you to not want to work with me anymore? Because I can stop explaining before we hit that point."

Colby shook his head. "My family's rich. You having a little magical side-business is not the weirdest thing I've ever been exposed to. Although...did you actually open the door with your brain?"

Okay, this isn't what I expected. "I don't know if it was my brain or not, but I opened it."

Colby smiled, and when he laughed that time, it wasn't a

half-chuckle, but a full, open-mouthed laugh that showed off those perfect white teeth and the pink of his tongue, and stretched his facial muscles taut and moved along the corded tendons in his neck. His hair rustled around his face. "See? I told you you were more interesting than the math brains I deal with back at school."

"You're really not freaking?"

"Why would I freak out about this? Who doesn't want magic to be real? As long as you promise not to turn me into a frog."

"It doesn't really work like that." It wasn't that Lachlan was ashamed of the magical dealings, or that he even thought it necessarily needed to remain a secret. But separating the businesses, that was a huge deal. Something his father and his grandmother had both been exceptionally clear about: don't mix the two. The candy shop clientele weren't meant to know that he could do anything out of the ordinary, because then they might not trust him to treat their candy purchase with sanctity. And it was true, he could easily manipulate a lot of the candies if that was something he chose to pursue. Hell, they even had a few family recipes specifically for it. Lozenges to get someone to share your bed. Lollipops that would give your enemies nightmares. Euphoria-inducing caramel. He'd snuck into the shop and made those at least six times when he was a teenager. Weed may not have been legal at the time, but nobody could say shit about the candy shop owner's son walking around with a bag of soft, luscious caramels.

"So…what actually happened, there?" Colby prodded the damp pile of boxers on the table. "Did you curse her to do bad laundry or was that actually about her husband?"

"Actually about her husband. She was supposed to come in yesterday, never showed, and then she begged me for something this morning. I gave her what I could on short notice, but apparently she's displeased with the truth." It was a hazard of the job, and why he definitely always took payment up front. Too often, a spell would pan out exactly the way it was meant to, and that would lead to the client coming back and giving him what for. But at least he had her money for the work he definitely did right. "It's not the first time someone's slapped me when things didn't go their way, but she could have at least taken her rings off." Lachlan reached up and touched his cheek, and came away with some blood. "Crap."

"It's not too bad. You'll come away with some rugged, manly scars from your treacherous battle."

"Yes, well... Sorry you had to see that whole thing go down."

"A slap fight over magic because her husband's cheating on her and she doesn't like it? You need to stop apologizing for providing me with a good time. People watch soap operas specifically because this stuff never happens in real life."

Lachlan mustered a tiny smile, but he still felt cold, in spite of the growing warm handprint on his left cheek. "I really hate when I have to give bad news like that, though. And especially with it being in front of a stranger. I tried to get her to head back for a reason." For multiple reasons, but protecting her pride had certainly been on the list.

Colby stood up and grabbed him by the shoulders. His eyes, dark and drawing, burned as he looked into Lachlan. "What can I do to help?"

"To help?"

"Is there something?" Colby's cheeks were pinkening again, but he never broke away from that intense eye contact. "I'm not going to lie, I'm out of my depth in a whole lot of ways, here, but if you feel bad...I don't know, would me running down the road and buying you some booze help?"

And in spite of himself, for all his good efforts to the contrary, Lachlan sputtered out a laugh. It refused to stay locked up behind even his tightest of pursed lips, and he rather embarrassingly may have sprayed spit all over Colby's very up-close-and-personal face. "Shit, I'm sorry. And for cussing. Sorry for that, too." He ducked behind the counter and grabbed a cloth, then handed it over. "There's a bathroom right over here."

"It's fine." Colby laughed as well as he rubbed his glasses with the cloth. "I'll be right back out. Then we can bring up the booze again?"

As Colby walked away, Lachlan let his eyes wander downward, taking in the work Colby said he'd put in on his glutes. And yeah, it definitely *had* paid off. Taut little buns that filled out his jeans maybe a little too nicley. Nicely enough that the animal core in Lachlan's stomach growled and clawed and purred into his mind about how nice it would be to reach out and take a feel, check out just how well those squats or lunges or whatever had really worked out. And that purred suggestion led to a tingling growth down between his legs. Not entirely *unwelcome,* but not fruitful. He grabbed the underwear from the table and took them back to his magic room. He didn't bother with the brazier for this volume of burning, pulled out the large pot he kept stored for larger situations just like this. Scorch marks lined the whole outside of the dull, silvery pot. Years of use. He tossed the underwear in, along with some seawater and a few quartz crystals, to purify it out. The last thing he wanted was a bunch of magical remnants hanging around his life.

He carried the pot into the kitchen proper, added enough water to just cover the boxers—not the weirdest thing he'd disposed of in this pot over the years—then whacked it on the heat. As high as it could go. It would boil off, the quartz and the seawater would take out any mystical impurities that would attempt to linger, and then the boxers would dry out and he'd take them out and burn them completely.

"That's not candy for the party, is it?" Colby walked back in, polishing his glasses on the cloth once more. He stopped just in the doorway to the kitchen, not setting foot over the actual threshold. "There's a lot of flavors I'm willing to try, but random lady's husband's crotch funk might be a bit over the line, even for me."

"No. But here." Lachlan grabbed some of the new batch of brittle he'd made. "Try this."

Colby took the translucent red shard and snapped some off with his front teeth. "Whoa." Immediately, Colby's eyes lit up. "You were right. It needed tweaking. This is great."

Lachlan stood a little taller at that comment. *Amazing what a compliment from a cute guy can do.*

"So, how about that booze?"

"I think I'm good. But thanks. I'm just going to throw myself into my work. If I do a good job for you, that'll get the bad taste out of my mouth."

Colby smiled at him. "I'll let you get to work, then. Unless you need me to stick around for anything?" He raised his hands in a mock fisticuffs stance. "I'm small, but I'm scrappy. In case anyone else wants to come and give you problems."

Lachlan smiled back, then focused on Colby's glasses and knocked them down to the tip of his nose. Another twitch of the head and they came off and descended gently to the table-top. "Think I can manage myself, but I'll keep you on speed dial in case I need backup."

Colby picked his glasses up and nodded. "I'll see you later, then. I might have to swing by later and pick up some more candy." He stepped toward the door, then turned around on his heel. "Crap. I forgot. Do you need a deposit for this? It's a big order."

I should. Given the giant reminder he'd just gotten about how useful that up front payment was, he really, really should have. But their conversation had been so nice. Colby hadn't freaked about the magic. And damn it, he was cute and that maybe shouldn't have entered into any kind of calculus, but it did. If he put down a deposit, what reason did he have to make another appearance? "You're a Grayson. I trust that you're going to be able to pay."

Colby shrugged. "Your funeral if the stock market explodes, I guess." And *then* he left. And Colby couldn't help the cheesy thought that passed through his mind. *Hate to see him go, but love to watch him leave.* And honestly, Lachlan did hate to see him go, at least a little bit. He liked the company, and he frankly didn't get a lot of chances to spend that much time with people anymore. The candy shop, and his worries about the candy shop, took up a lot of his time, and aside from that, Cape Elizabeth didn't necessarily have a *ton* of options for gay dating. Not that it was particularly frowned upon. He knew of at least a dozen same-sex couples who lived in Cape Elizabeth. But that was just it. They were couples. As far as Lachlan knew, there were a handful of single floating queer folks in the area, and the nearest gay bar was only twenty minutes away, but twenty minutes was practically a cross-country journey when he was exhausted and sticky from sugar work, or smelling of smoke and sage and saltwater from some spell.

Plus, frankly, the thought of driving all the way into Portland, then being rejected? Lachlan damn sure didn't want to deal with that. And he had a history of getting rejected. Hence how he was still single and only had a one-night stand about once a year. Normally on his birthday, because come on. He deserved sex on his *birthday* if he deserved it *ever*.

So yeah, he was a little forlorn that he'd be working the rest of the time in the shop alone.

But he'd make it through. The little whisper of Colby's citric cologne still lingering on the air helped make it a little less lonely.

Lachlan hadn't felt this immediate sting of infatuation in years. A welcome reminder that he was still able to feel those things, that those bits of him hadn't sloughed off from lack of attention, but also inevitably fleeting. Like seeing an attractive newcomer behind a booth at some convention somewhere, or taking in the muscular biceps of the guy who farmed his own produce for the farmer's market, it was lovely, and it would stabilize out like it always did.

But he could leverage those feelings while they lasted. He could ride the high of the dopamine for a while, and produce some damn good candy, and deliver it to the wealthy folks who would inevitably be present at the Grayson Halloween gala. *And if I happen to leave very clear directions for how to get to my website, what's that going to hurt?*

Rubbing his hands together, Lachlan darted back into the kitchen. The smell of boiling boxers and seawater had faded now, and he could get to work. He was meant to play with his flavors for this job? "Let's see where we can work in some rosewater." Rich people loved eating shit like flowers. It just so happened that Lachlan did, too. A chance to realistically play with such a weird little under-appreciated ingredient? He'd take that every day and twice on Sundays.

CHAPTER FOUR

*L*achlan worked all through the day. A couple customers actually did slip inside and buy some taffy, some gummies. Little things, amounting to relatively little profit. But he wasn't complaining. End of day, he had a new large-batch order online. More likely than not for a wedding or a baby shower or something like that. Otherwise, why would anyone need five pounds of candy-coated walnuts in pastel blue? Still, those were easy enough. He'd only have to devote a couple hours total to the nuts, which would leave him plenty of time to keep up and continue his testing for Colby's order. The rosewater pastilles had worked remarkably well, so he was mostly set on keeping that recipe as it was, so long as he could replicate the same results again. He also had a few less ambitious candies, standbys that he knew would work, and wouldn't alienate the folks who weren't too keen on trying the licorice and rhubarb chews he was working on. They needed a lot more rhubarb, and a lot less licorice, but he was confident the idea could actually *work*. He just needed time and experimentation. It may well end up being an after-hours project for him, or even one he tried to play with in his home kitchen, sans all the usual equipment.

The next day, he showed up at his usual time, but had to head out to the grocery store to pick up some standard ingredients. Cream, butter, eggs. The sort of thing he didn't buy straight from candy suppliers. When he got back, he was shocked to see a familiar, slim-featured figure. Colby was there, replete once again with coffee, and wearing another oversized sweater that threatened to swallow him up, but this time in solid black. He had on cream-colored chinos, straight-legged, and currently stared down at his phone. His breath puffed visibly in the autumnal chill.

"You know I don't actually open for another hour and a half, right?"

Colby jerked his head up. His lenses had turned half-foggy from the breath bouncing up into his face from the phone screen. But he smiled all the same, slipping them off to wipe them clean. "If it's a problem, I can leave. But…well, frankly, I don't particularly want to spend time with the family when there's a far more interesting candymaker not too far away from home."

Am I insane to think he's flirting? "I promise I'm not that interesting." Lachlan slipped past Colby, unlocked the door, and ushered him in. "But I can at least let you get the chill out of your bones." He'd put his displays back in order after Colby had left the day before, so the shop was fully restored to its normal state. "And if you keep bringing me coffee, I'll have to knock money off your order."

"Then I'll just have to tip you to make up the difference. My family's rich. I can win this fight."

Lachlan chuckled, taking the latte with his name scrawled across the side. Another pumpkin spice, the fragrance wafting up as he brought it close to his nose. "I'm not going to fight *that* hard for you to not pay me."

"Good." Colby sighed and clapped his hands against his hips. "So, is there some way I can make myself useful here?"

"I'm pretty good. Need to come in and do some recipe dev more than anything." Lachlan walked back and tucked his perishables away, then headed back out front for a final spit and polish on the storefront. Checking and rechecking that he had everything in place to handle walk-ins, making sure his displays looked as nice as possible, as enticing as he could get them. He also marked down which jars and bins could use a topping up. Not many, but now and then he had to empty out old stock, and he'd been selling here and there a bit more. Not to the level he'd expected for Halloween, the level he needed in order to feel comfortable, but more.

Then he headed in to do mise en place for the day. "I can let you back, but you can't really touch anything, and you have to keep your distance. Or wear a hair net." Colby's hair was lovely, but it would be considerably less lovely to see it fall into a batch of molten sugar he'd have to completely toss out.

Colby held out his hand. "Net me up."

Okay, then. Lachlan pulled out one of the disposable hairnets and handed it over. Colby actually put it on like he knew what he was doing, too, making sure to tuck all his loose ends in, then went immediately to scrub up his hands, rolling his sleeves up so he could wash his forearms. "You worked in a kitchen before?"

"Another thing from my mom. She wanted me to work a service job at some point so I could understand it. I was a dishwasher for six months, then got moved up to serving at the buffet." He dried off on one of the clean, white towels. "So yeah, I know what I'm doing a little bit."

"Sounds like your mom was worried about you getting big-headed."

"A little bit. I'm happy for it, though. We associate mostly with other families who have the same kind of money." He blushed a little bit, but didn't turn his eyes away. "I don't like to speak ill of others when I don't have to, but some of their children are *not* the kind of people I'd want to associate with. At least a few of them actually mocked me when they saw me working a job, like that was ridiculous."

"Dicks?"

"Little bit of dicks, yeah. Sometimes." Colby sighed. "Okay, is it better if I stand completely out of the way, or stay here?"

Lachlan chuckled. "Maybe just stick back a little bit, but you can stay close. It'll be good to get your input on your own order, anyway."

"Ooh, taste-testing."

Lachlan nodded and started cracking and separating eggs. "I need to get these nuts done up for an order first, but they won't take long."

They stayed quiet for a while. Colby seemed happy to simply stand there, spending time in the kitchen, sipping his coffee. Lachlan made quick work of the candy coating, tinting the fluffy, sugary mixture a pale blue before mixing in the walnut meats. Then they went into the oven to dry out for an hour or so. He had to be careful with them, especially given that the color request was so pale. If he let them get too hot, they'd discolor and ruin the whole effect. So low, low, low and slow was the only way to really go this time around. Then it was time to start on the actual big order, and suddenly Lachlan felt a hell of a lot more self-conscious about this whole thing. He went for his candy oils and located the mint. *Mint for calming and nausea.* He took the cap off and inhaled deeply, his sinuses immediately opening. Three deep breaths. Not all witchy things were inherently magical. Sometimes, it was just knowing how different substances could affect you.

"Is it going to be better if I head out?"

Lachlan turned around and faced Colby. "What?"

"You're used to doing this all alone, right? Are you

wanting to be alone while you do this work? I mean, you seem like you're really anxious right now."

"That obvious?"

"To be fair, I don't have much else to do at this precise moment than watch you. So maybe not obvious, but a little obvious." He smiled at Lachlan, pushing his cheeks up. A broad, full smile, markedly not restrained like he had been in the past. Did it make Lachlan's knees a little quivery to be under the full, complete ministrations of that brilliant smile, those dark eyes that demanded he come forward and fall into their depths?

Perhaps. Perhaps it did. Lachlan would plead the fifth.

"I think I just need to relax a little. Nervous. You're good, though." *Let's get going. We still need more brittle. Start there.* He started the roasting on his pumpkin seeds, then began to melt down the sugar in a big, steel-clad aluminum pot. "You just have to promise not to judge me for all this."

"Judge you? For what? I'm not a candy maker."

"Yeah, but I'm still developing the recipes for your party in a lot of cases. It's like a painter debuting the sketches to the client instead of the finished project."

Colby nodded. "I really can go."

That wasn't what Lachlan wanted at all. *The problem is that I want two totally different things.* He liked Colby, found him massively interesting. And hot. And interesting. Hot and interesting went together rarely, but very, very well. But also, Lachlan needed to get the work done, which apparently wasn't about to happen while Colby was standing there.

Really, there was only one actual answer that could work, here, even if it twisted Lachlan's stomach into knots and immediately dried out his throat.

He turned his back to Colby and focused on the slowly dissolving sugar in the pot, watching the gentle honey-amber color creep across pure white crystals. Maybe if he didn't look, it would be easier to make his tongue function. "What are you doing later? Maybe I can get some of the kinks worked out with this, and then we can…meet up somewhere? I'll bring samples."

"Hey, that works for me. Where's somewhere?"

"Wherever, really. I was thinking a restaurant here in town? Dealer's choice. Or my place." *Why the hell did I say that?*

"Your place would be good."

Lachlan finally looked over at Colby again, reacting before he even recognized what had drawn his attention so quickly. Seeing Colby suddenly withdrawn, gaze drawn down, solidified what it was. A tiny catch he'd noticed in Colby's voice, a slightly higher, frantic pitch than his usual gentle tenor, a quickened pace to his words. Some sort of nerves, caused by…what? Lachlan was a witch, not a psychic. "We don't have to."

"No, no." Again, Colby spoke too fast, and his eyes darted upward again. "It's good. Just caught by surprise." He sighed, slipping his glasses off and polishing them down on the bottom of his sweater. Lachlan couldn't help but notice the tiny flash of skin, the gray waistband of his underwear peeking up above his chinos. He wasn't necessarily *proud* of the fact that he took note of that, but he definitely took note of it, the flatness of the skin, the way he got a stupid hormonal thrill at the sight of it, the way his mind questioned how warm it would feel under his fingertips.

When Colby had slipped his glasses back on, he seemed slightly more regulated. Enough that he gave off that half-cocked smile, the tiny, muted chuckle again. "Not every day such a good-looking guy invites me back to his place."

It was apparently Lachlan's turn to blush, as the heat rising through his chest and up his throat wasn't from the heat of the sugar melting away. "It's not every day I get to *invite* such a good-looking guy up to my place." This for sure was flirting. No insanity necessary. Right? It sure as hell felt like it, as much as Lachlan could actually *remember* what flirting felt like. He was being called hot by this guy who was definitely 100% admittedly into guys. No, this was absolutely flirting.

Lachlan fished out his phone and shot off a quick text. "I just gave you my address." *We're doing this.* "Sorry about kind of pushing you out the door."

"Hey, I offered to head out." Caleb slipped off his hairnet and tossed it into the trash bin next to the door. "Does six o'clock work for you?"

I can shower and everything by then. "Yep. I hope you can survive until then."

"I'm very sure. It's not bad. You're just better." Colby headed out, then immediately the doors swung back open. "Wine. Do you drink wine, or would bringing a bottle be a waste?"

"Business wine?"

Colby nodded without a moment's hesitation. "If you're going to continue to spend time with the upper crust, you'll get used to drinking over business. It's how we do everything."

And Lachlan couldn't quite hold back his tongue. "Is that why rich people make so many bad decisions?"

But instead of being offended, Colby gave that half-chuckle. "Liberal application of Barolo and French champagne may have been involved in my uncle once buying one thousand shares of a seaweed farm in Michigan."

"In Michigan? Doesn't seaweed normally require the sea?"

Colby nodded. "You see how easy that is to realize when you're sober? He didn't put that together until the day after the contract had been signed. He's never quite had a taste for champagne since." Colby patted the door frame and gave a final nod. "I'll see you tonight."

And he was gone, leaving only a whiff of citrus in his wake.

CHAPTER FIVE

business meeting didn't usually take this sort of prep work. *I should have asked him to come at six thirty.* He'd so far managed to straighten up his house, which had looked a little too much like a frat house for his liking, and was just now getting out of the shower with ten minutes to spare. His hair was still wet, and he was scrubbing his pits dry when the doorbell rang.

For a brief, slightly embarrassing moment, Lachlan had a vision of himself answering with just a towel wrapped around his waist and...well, he'd maybe watched one too many pornos if his head was going there.

Lachlan quickly slipped into his trunks, then fresh jeans and a heather gray T-shirt. He was halfway across the living room when the doorbell rang again.

Lachlan opened the door and was met with Colby, a bottle of sparkling wine, and the edge of his tag sticking up on the bottom of his vision, because he'd somehow managed to put his shirt on inside out and backwards. "Hey."

"I'm not too early, am I?"

"No. I just got out of the shower." Lachlan reached up and twiddled his shirt tag. "If you can't tell." He stepped aside and gestured Colby through the door. "You can set that in the kitchen. I'm just going to go dress like I actually know what I'm doing."

And Lachlan darted off to his bathroom, quickly swapping his shirt around. He took a few extra seconds to look in the mirror, whispering fiercely to his own reflection. "It's a business meeting. Flirtation is flirtation. And maybe this is flirtation. But it's also business. And the business is more important. But I guess if it comes around to flirtation, that's fine." He knew he should stop and actually go out and spend time with his guest, but it seemed so much simpler to just keep chattering away at himself. He grabbed a brush to run through his hair to occupy himself a little bit more. "I did ask him if he wanted to get together, and I felt weird about it, so I knew what I was intending. I guess I wasn't intending on drinking with him in close proximity to a couch and a bed and table and all sorts of other flat, horizontal surfaces." He hadn't had a babble session like this in quite a while. Normally, this kind of incessant self-talk only happened when he had to deal with his family. *So nerves. Yay.*

Finally, he couldn't realistically stay in the bathroom changing his shirt without raising alarms about his general well-being, so Lachlan stepped back out. Colby was at the counter, not touching the two stuffed green candy boxes, but hovering very close by, with the wine bottle sitting aside next to it.

"They're your samples, you can try them whenever you want."

Colby glanced at him. "Well, if you insist."

This, Lachlan could deal with perfectly fine. Colby lifted the lids off the boxes, revealing about two dozen different little, labeled sections inside, each filled with a different confection. "Can I swear?"

"You're a big boy, I think you can swear."

"Holy shit, you outdid yourself."

"Well, several of them are candies I already had made. Some standbys that I think will go over well." He shifted closer, sliding into the aura of his bright, lovely cologne. He pointed to different candies as he talked about them. "This is just honeycomb with dark chocolate and salt." Lachlan was *not* a chocolatier by any stretch of even the wildest imagination. That little dip into some dark chocolate amounted for half the chocolate in his shop. "These piña coloda ones here are lollipops, but I left the sticks out to get them to fit better. And these are those little clove ones that you had that first day. Figured I would move those into the rotation."

Colby snatched up one of the faded green gummies and popped it into his mouth. "Definitely keep those." Then he scoured his eyes across the various creations. He stopped at some puffy white things, each maybe half an inch long and wrapped in wax paper. "Are these taffy?"

"Just a basic divinity. I'm not sure about that one, to be honest. I love it, but it can get a little messy for the upper crust folks I'm cooking for this time around." He grabbed one and peeled the paper away, revealing a light, fluffy confection studded through with chopped pecans. It didn't stick too badly to the wax paper, but still left a bit of residue behind. His fingers were where it was worst, covering them in tiny white filaments of sugar and egg white. "I made more than I actually intend to cook up for the party, that way there's room to cut things out."

Colby took one himself, unwrapped it, and popped it past his lips. He also sucked the sweetness off his fingers, which did horribly uncomfortable, welcome, unhelpful things to Lachlan. "That's really good, but you're probably right. Fashion being what it is."

Lachlan nodded and ate his own divinity. Light, sticky, strong vanilla flavor. It wasn't something he could actually stock all that easily at the shop. Sugar was already hygroscopic, and sugar with a different kind of liquid sugar *and* egg whites, out here on the coast? Yeah, that was a recipe for messy weeping all over the place. Plus he'd have to find some way to use a full day's stock of divinity each day, and frankly his hips wouldn't appreciate quite that many calories injected into his diet. He damn sure knew his jeans wouldn't appreciate it.

"Well, I need to pace myself on candy, anyway." Colby grabbed the bottle of wine and, without even a moment's hesitation, removed the cage from the top and began twisting it. The cork slipped free remarkably fast, with only the tiniest of hisses instead of a big, messy pop. "Do you have wine glasses, or are we going Bohemian for the evening?"

"That's a nice way of saying ratchet." Lachlan slipped past Colby, unavoidably drawing in the scent of him, and accidentally brushing against the back of his sweater and feeling the impossibly soft material against the back of his hand. He didn't comment on it, just pulled out a pair of smallish water glasses. They weren't even chipped.

"Frankly, we use too much fancy crap. Do you know the purpose of a champagne flute?" Colby poured the pale, bubbling wine halfway up each glass, stopping just short enough that, as it fizzed, the bubbles crested the top without spilling over.

"The smaller surface area of a champagne flute makes fewer bubbles, so it doesn't go flat so fast."

Colby stopped. "Really? I was just going to go off about how it was so we could all look fancier and spend even more money on yet another specialized wine glass."

"I'm in the food industry, even if it is just candy. So yeah, that's the real reason." Lachlan took one of the glasses and raised it high. "Just means we'll have to drink this faster to avoid losing the bubbles."

"Cheers to that." Colby clinked his glass, then raised it to his lips and took a small drag. His lips glistened slightly when he pulled his drink away. "So, can I ask you something?"

"Sure."

"Why are you helping me get out of the house like this? I'm just a client."

"I mean, if that's how you want to describe yourself. Frankly, you're the most interesting person I've gotten to talk to around here in a decade." Maybe that was a bit of an overstatement, but still. A nice thing to say, and not entirely without merit. He definitely made the top five.

"I'm just the son of some rich family taking a boring degree."

"Boring degree? Figuring out how to handle money? That sounds great to me, and you said already you like math."

Colby offered up the half chuckle and took another, deeper drink. "Still, do you often take clients back home? Or tell them how attractive they are?"

"I think you started that one." Lachlan took a hearty gulp of bubbling wine. Nice and dry, crisp and acidic. If he hadn't been covering for his own nerves, he'd have mightily enjoyed this particular wine, complimented Colby on it. As it stood, he just needed a higher blood alcohol content, and something to occupy himself with while he reeled from his sudden shock of boldness.

"I may have." Colby was going pink in the cheeks again. "But it's mostly because I can't lie for crap."

"Not telling me that wouldn't have been lying."

Colby nodded. "Yeah, but you're hot. And I wanted you to know that *I* knew you were hot."

Okay, I wasn't expecting this at all. So Lachlan drank again, even though he was draining wine out at an alarming rate by this point. "Thanks?"

Colby smiled. "I don't know what the hell, to be honest. I don't act like this, but...have you looked at yourself in a mirror before?"

"Yeah. I have one weird, long nose hair, a mole under my left nipple, and a shitty tattoo on my ribs that some guy named Orange Juice did in the back of his minivan when I was eighteen."

Colby laughed, and it was full, and it shook his whole body, and he even had to set his drink down. And as he laughed, Lachlan couldn't help joining in. Maybe it was the wine. Maybe it was being in close proximity to such unbridled laughter. Maybe it was simply that, whatever Colby had to say about Lachlan, Colby was the hot one here, and Lachlan just wanted to be on his good side.

After nearly a minute of laughing, trying to catch his breath, and busting out again, Colby wiped his eyes. "I'm sorry about that. I don't know why, that just took me by surprise." He finished off what remained of the pale sparkling wine. "Did you actually get a tattoo from a guy named Orange Juice? Where do you even meet a guy named Orange Juice. Or a gal named Orange Juice. Or an enby named Orange Juice, even. Just an *individual* named after a breakfast beverage."

Lachlan smiled as he settled back into the memory. And he liked the idea of sharing it. It was one of his better tales. "Living room?"

"I'm bringing the candy. And the wine."

Lachlan chuckled and grabbed one of the boxes of candy. Colby took the other and the bottle and they headed for the modest sitting area near the front door. Lachlan always wished he could redecorate it a little bit, but money being what it was, he just had the loveseat and a low, slightly chipped, roughed up coffee table. But at least at the moment, the somewhat tight confines of the floral-patterned loveseat weren't the worst thing.

Colby settled in, and while there was space between them, Lachlan could definitely feel the heat of his hip radiating against him. His lungs filled with the bright, citric cologne as it mingled with the effervescence of the wine.

Colby nodded and grabbed another clove gummy. "So, tell me about Orange Juice."

Lachlan sighed and sipped his wine in preparation. "So I was eighteen, shouldn't have been out drinking obviously, but I was gay and depressed and mad at my dad, seeing as how he's a huge asshole and all."

"Is he really, or is that teenage stuff?"

"No, he's actually a giant dick. So I was out with some friends, and at the time my friend Sheila was dating this bartender who had some weird sketchy friends."

"One of whom happened to be named Orange Juice?"

Lachlan nodded. "I'm pretty sure his real name was Jeremy or Jason or Jackson. Something like that. I guess they called him Orange Juice because he was on the wagon, but him and all his buddies would hit the bar in the morning. They were on night shift. And he'd order a virgin screwdriver. Anyway, he'd tried to be a tattoo artist while he was still drinking, but gave up. Still had the machine, and he decided to bring that and some ink to this beach party drinking thing we were having."

"That seems irresponsible."

"Super irresponsible. That's what made it so appealing. I had a few tequila sunrises in my belly, and Sheila was continually making them stronger as the evening went on. And I decided fuck it, I want to get some kind of gay tattoo while I have the chance. Orange Juice thought it was a great idea. He charged me the crappy necklace I used to wear back then. Just a little beaded yellow and black choker that I guarantee was too small for his neck. So off with my shirt, lying down in the back of Orange Juice's van."

"Is that sanitary?"

"Again, do you think that crossed my mind? He did his best in the circumstances. The needles he used were all fresh and in the wrapper, and he soaped down where he was going to put the ink. He wore gloves. All that."

"That's better than just dipping the needles in a vat of hepatitis, but still."

"Hey, I'm not recommending anyone follow in my foot-steps. Besides, it's really not great. You can sort of tell what it is, but not from a distance."

Colby sighed. "Well come on. I'm not listening to this horror story and then *not* getting to actually see the ink."

And with the wine and the proximity and them already both teetering on the edge, Lachlan didn't—or perhaps couldn't—hold his tongue back. "You came up to my apart-ment. Aren't I supposed to convince you to undress?"

Colby smiled, shrugged, and tucked his arms into his sleeves. The sweater came up and over his head as time slowed in the general vicinity of the living room. Lachlan watched as his flat tummy was revealed, then his pecs, carved gently against his slender form. His ribs stood out visibly, but not worryingly so. A scar ran along his right biceps, and on the left was a small, violet lambda. Much subtler and much better-done than Lachlan's "I'm a young homosexual" tattoo.

Colby sighed, folding his shirt roughly and setting it aside. He tapped his glasses, knocked askew by the removal of the sweater, back into place on the bridge of his nose. "There. I've been convinced." He reached over and refilled his glass with wine, acting all nonchalant even as the pink hit his cheeks and, now that he was exposed, Lachlan saw it starting down at the base of his throat. Just the tiniest tinge of rosiness.

"You were pretty easy to convince."

"We're both adults, right? And it's not like either of us were all that subtle about what we wanted, right?" He took a drink, but a tiny quiver of his hand clinked the glass against the coffee table as he set it back down. "So? I'm not showing off my nipples for free. I need to see this tatt."

"Well, since you insist." Lachlan stood and rolled his shoulders back, then took his shirt off yet again. He didn't bother folding it up, just tossed it over the back of the loveseat. Then he turned his right side to Colby and lifted up his arm. "It's supposed to be, you know, two Mars symbols interlocked."

"It's not *not* that." Colby actually got up and moved closer, close enough that his bare-chested heat radiated out against Lachlan's own exposed torso. "It's also not *not* a pair of cartoon legs, like someone's swimming down into your kidney. Definitely could have been done better."

"Yeah, let's just say that I don't plan on going back to Orange Juice if I can eventually get this thing covered up."

Colby nodded. "What do you want to cover it with?"

"Well, it's small enough that I have options. Maybe some kind of flowers? I think black and white roses could be cute, right? Not super looking forward to getting my ribs tattooed again, but it is what it is."

"Oh, yeah, ribs probably sucked, huh?"

"I was drunk and I still hated it. Sober doesn't sound like any fun at all."

He kept waiting for Colby to back away, for them to sit there together, shirtless, talking, unsure what to do going forward. But instead, Colby straightened up, not backing away at all. "So this is a weird, awkward question, but can I touch your abs? Like, you actually have some."

"Like, two."

"Like six, stop being modest when I can see them right in front of my own face with my own eyes."

"I'd compromise at four. But you can touch them." The sentence nearly caught on his throat, not ready to come out unimpeded. "Count for yourself."

Time continued to slow, even as Lachlan's heart beat in his ears. This wasn't the sort of person he was. Not that there was any issue with having casual encounters. It just wasn't his everyday setting, so to be this close to some hottie, telling him to have at it, touch him, just completely out of nowhere... yeah, it was a thrill, and a sinking in his stomach, and somehow still so correct, but simultaneously ethereal in the extreme, as though he was asleep and this was nothing but some passing fancy that would break apart as soon as he felt the brush of those fingertips against his stomach. He even braced for it as he watched Colby reaching down.

Yet nothing shattered. Time rubberbanded back into normalcy beneath the too-soft ministrations of Colby's fingertips. They brushed gently over the skin, over the slight trail of hair that led down beneath his waistband. Colby was too low, his breath warm against Lachlan's navel, and he struggled to shift himself in place, trying to hide his very non-socially-acceptable semi growing to fruition in his jeans. *Is it bad to get one? That's what we're doing, right? Isn't it?*

"One. Two. Three." Each number came as an explosion of damp heat against Lachlan's midsection, paired up with the gentle tap and scrape of a finger and nail. "Four. Five. Six. And I'm a finance major, so I know my numbers." He stood up and looked Lachlan in the eye. "While I was down there, I couldn't help but notice...you know."

"Sorry."

"Don't be sorry. I'm flattered. I should apologize a little bit, though. I don't want to fool around. We're still mostly strangers."

"Oh."

"I mean, I want to." The pink went to a full-fledged flush across Colby's chest, neck, and face. "I really, really want to." He made a furtive gesture to his own crotch by way of explanation. "But I don't think we should."

"It's not professional, I know."

"No, I'm a bottom and I didn't prep because I knew if I let it happen as fast as it could, we'd go at supersonic speeds. Or at least I would. So I took precautions."

"So if you had prepped…"

"I'd happily be on my back clutching my ankles and shouting obscenities to the deity of your choice right now." Colby shook his head, his cheeks flushing darker and darker pink. "I'm trying really hard not to feel weird about this whole thing."

"You and me both. It's…really fast, right?"

"That's the rub, isn't it?" Colby chuckled. "More wine?"

Lachlan nodded, and got his glass refilled. "So, I'm a little confused by what the plan is."

"The plan? You're fucking hot and we're in your apartment, and if you asked for head, I'd be on my knees in an instant."

"That's…good to know. But if you don't want to do that, then what are we doing here?"

"Gauging interest, getting a peek at what's to come, and getting to have a harmless good time."

Lachlan looked him up and down, took in the expanse of all that warm skin, the tiny flashes of coarse, dark hair peeking out from his armpits. "The pleasure's mine."

"So…can I go total nerd on this whole situation for a second?" Colby slipped off his glasses and reached down to polish them up on the shirt he was no longer wearing. Then he reached for his folded sweater and used that instead. "Or would me talking all clinical really bring down the mood?"

"If we're not fooling around, I think maybe bringing down the mood might be a good call for the both of us." Although either way, Lachlan had a suspicion he'd be getting a second shower in tonight to handle this particular "mood."

"So, I figure I'm going to explode if this doesn't get resolved in short order." Colby nodded and made the little half-chuckle again. "But, you know, I have history of throwing myself at guys and it's explosive and fizzles out. And at least while I'm here, I'd like to spend time with you.

You're interesting and hot and gay and talented. Don't interrupt to try and be modest, either."

"Wouldn't dream of it."

"So…I'm inviting you to the Halloween party. You'll be able to meet up with people, be the face of all the fucking delicious candy at the party. Sorry, I cuss a lot more when I'm drinking. But then also, if we still want to…you know. Well, then I'll prep and we can go at it like rabbits on Viagra." For the first time since the whole spiel started, Colby looked up at him, brows knitting together in the middle. "So is that too controlling and nerdy and exacting?"

Lachlan smiled and took a heavy swig of wine. "Well, let's see. You make all the plans. You introduce me to a bunch of new potential clients with a shit ton of money. And I know that come Halloween, as long as I'm not boring or a dick between then and now, I get laid? I don't know how I'll survive."

"It's just, I know it kind of sucks the spontaneity out of things."

"Spontaneous anal is a recipe for a bad time and a lot of dry cleaning."

Colby let loose another complete, encompassing peal of laughter, and with his sweater off, Lachlan could see the way it flexed his abdominal muscles, tightened up his biceps, turned the already pronounced lines of corded muscle in his neck to steel cables for those few seconds. If Lachlan hadn't been hardening up already, he would have popped straight to attention like some overly hormonal teenager.

Colby locked eyes with him, still smiling. "Speaking from experience?"

"I'm not nearly drunk enough, or close enough with you, to go into sex horror stories. That would take hard liquor, and I don't even know how much. But I will say I was the top, and he tried to warn me."

"I don't think *I'm* drunk enough for you to tell any more

of that story." But still, Colby was grinning broad. "So, now that I'm all loosened up, let's get into critiquing your candy."

"Hmm, one stipulation." What the hell? If they were going to be playing these flirty, sexy games with each other, he may as well push his luck a little bit. Besides, Colby was looking entirely too comfortable, and he needed to experience the sort of *excitement* that he'd inflicted on Lachlan. "You got to feel me up. Turnabout's fair play."

Colby blinked a few times, then eventually nodded and stood. "All right. I'm not one to play unfair games."

There were so many options. Lachlan had one to decide on. The flat of his belly? The slight groove running along the side of his navel, down beneath his jeans? Go for broke and smack him on the ass?

In the end, he sidled up, got right in close to Colby, and leaned his head to the side. Then he found the pulsing jugular and pressed his lips gently to it, feeling the rush of livelihood just beneath the skin. He lingered a few moments, smelling the rush of that cologne on the pulse point as Colby's breath hitched.

He pulled back and slid back onto the loveseat. "There."

"That's not exactly an equivalent exchange."

"Did anyone *tell you* that you couldn't have kissed each of my abs while you were counting?"

Colby rolled his eyes and sat back down next to him, this time not taking any care to stay separated. Denim on denim, hip to hip. "You keep playing games like that, there's no way I'm going to make it to Halloween."

"It's your plan. Edit as needed." This wine was stopping any suggestion of a barrier around what Lachlan would usually say. It had created a direct river of sparkling bubbles from his thoughts to his lips. "So, tasting candy?"

"Right." Colby pulled one box over. "Walk me through these."

CHAPTER SIX

*L*achlan spent the next day alone, making candy based on Colby's notes from their evening together. Neither of them had wanted to part, or put clothes on, but it got late enough, and Colby got drunk enough, that it was either separate, or Colby was spending the night there. And there was only one bed in the house, which they both knew would lead to exactly one situation.

Four days until Halloween, and Lachlan had a solid set of recipes, could start making some of the heartier fare, the stuff that wouldn't break down or lose flavor or go soggy and weepy.

The second day after their evening at Lachlan's house, Colby walked back into the store. He was wearing that same bright, Missoni-esque sweater. Although, given how much money the Grayson's had, for all Lachlan knew it really was a Missoni. He was wearing that oversized sweater along with thin black gloves, a dark knit cap, and pale blue jeans studded with rivets from his hip bones all the way down to his ankles. And they were tight, and Lachlan wasn't religious, but he imagined God saying "and it was good."

Because damn was it good.

"I didn't bring coffee today." He slipped his hat off, releasing a mess of hair that bloomed around his face, then peeled off his gloves and shoved them into his jeans pockets. "It's *cold* out there."

"I've never had a Halloween in Cape Elizabeth that wasn't testicle-freezing, so I'm not surprised. Don't you come back here every year for this?"

"Yes, but I'm positive this is much colder than usual." He scrubbed his hands together, blowing down on them. "Either that or I'm used to California."

"Come back in the kitchen a second." Lachlan held the doors open for him. Once it was closed, Lachlan led him into the little magic room off the back. "Here. Cinnamon oil, cloves, and a little pine ash." He mixed them together in his tiny brazier, then struck the whole mixture alight with his fingertips. Once it was smoking good and billowy, he blew outward into the smoke plume so it enveloped Colby's middle. After it cleared, he doused the embers with a little bottle of water he kept on the back counter. "Better?"

"Yeah, actually. You're magic."

"Yep. Last time I checked."

"Just honestly gets lost in everything else about you."

Lachlan was pretty glad the room back here was dark, because that? That was a compliment that heated his face immediately. "I'm pretty sure the magic is a big deal."

"Not as big as the candymaking, or the fact that you know some guy named Orange Juice, or the way you talk about food, or...if I'm being shallow, your six-pack. But I think I mostly like how cut and dry you are."

"I'm not the one who laid out a fuck plan in my living room."

"I didn't say you were as cut and dry as I am. But a normal person wouldn't have acquiesced to the plan quite so easily." Colby smiled at him, his glasses glinting in the industrial fluorescents.

"Are you implying I'm not normal?"

"A candymaking gay witch boy? I don't feel like it's entirely unreasonable to suggest you're not normal."

In response, Lachlan nodded and knocked Colby's glasses down his nose again. "Point taken." He went back to the big pot bubbling away on the stove. The makings of his gummy base, since he had four different confections in this order that took it. "I know I kind of shuffled you out last time, but I kind of missed having you around yesterday. Now that I've got the recipes squared away pretty well, I don't mind the company."

"How much would you mind it if I counted your abs again?"

"I'd mind it as much as my client would. Which would be you. But also the health department if they decide to pay me a visit." Lachlan smiled at him. "And if I'm being a little selfish, I don't need molten sugar anywhere unpleasant. That's why I shave my arms."

"You shave your arms?"

"At least if the sugar splashes, it's not also catching in my arm hair and burning me even worse and even longer." He checked the temperature of the syrup. It was at a nice soft ball, so he took it off the burner. Which is when, somehow, there was the tinkling of bells. A customer. "Crap."

"Oh, do I get to be the assistant dealing with people?" Colby clapped his hands. "I'll occupy them until you can get this taken care of."

"Oh. Thanks." This situation didn't come up often, but he usually just handled it by shouting through the doors that he'd be a minute. Never caused any issues. But having someone to help was nice all the same. Still, he made quick work of separating the mixture out, stirring in the gelatin, then dividing, flavoring, and pouring the mixture into the prepared pans.

As he was just finishing up the flavor and color mixing, Colby came back in. "This guy is claiming that he has full rights to eat anything he wants, and that if I don't produce you out of the back, he's going to curse me and my grandchildren—"

"And your great grandchildren and all their ancestors with an infertility that will never cease so long as a drop of your blood remains in human veins?"

"That precisely, actually. Do you know him?"

Shit on a shingle. "Yeah. Wasn't expecting a visit from my dad, but…I guess see him back here." His dick of a father making a reappearance from whatever beach he'd been relaxing on wasn't exactly on his list of favorite things, but that was a classic threat when the asshole wasn't getting his way. Lachlan had never seen such a curse actually carried out, but he stuck with it anyway. *Old men retelling the same jokes until they die.*

"Lachlan!" The booming voice was all the further confirmation he needed.

Lachlan shifted his position around so he could make eye contact. "Dad."

Immediately, he was always struck by the similarities between himself and his father. He'd never really known his mother. She sent letters here and there, more when he was younger, but the same way that he and his dad sort of leaned into the candymaking side of the business, she'd gone full on witchy, was involved in some kind of weird, shady cabal of other magical folks who worked to try and…do something unspecified. She'd assured him in several letters over the years that they weren't after world domination, just the betterment of life quality for witches. She'd left not just because of that, of course. She'd also found his father just as insufferable as Lachlan did.

But judging from the pictures he'd seen of her, he'd inherited blond locks and slightly pointed ears from her. But everything else, from his broad shoulders to his angular jaw to the light brown eyes had come down from his father. Basically just a blond carbon copy, minus a few years.

"I see the place is just as empty as when I came six months ago."

"Yeah. I'm not blind yet."

His father's smile was forced, but practiced. Lachlan doubted if anyone unfamiliar with him would have been able to pick up on the falsehood of it. "You seem busy for having so many cobwebs in the corners."

"Got a big order I'm working on for a client." Rather than giving more than passing focus to his dad, he started mixing up the colored sugars for the various gummies. It needed to go on top now while they were still tacky, but set enough that it wouldn't dissolve or sink through. "You remember the Graysons. Grandma talks about their Halloween party all the time?"

"Oh really. You're working for the rich bitches, now."

Lachlan cringed at that and finally fixed his full, unbroken attention on his dad. "Their son happens to be the one who saw you back here, so maybe watch your mouth around clients." He glanced over his dad's shoulder and nodded to Colby. "Dad, that's Colby Grayson. Colby, my dad, Dorian James."

He looked over his shoulder as well. "Charmed." Then he was back on his son. "I'd like to see the books. Since you're doing so well with my shop, apparently."

"I'm a little busy."

"You think I can't find them?" He snapped and the lights all flicked off. Another snap and they came back. "I taught you everything you know, right?"

"Grandma taught me plenty. Research taught me plenty. Experimentation taught me plenty. And I still do hear from mom now and then." He transferred the pistachio-colored sugar into a shaker and started dusting over the top of the cloves gummies. "I wouldn't make any assumptions about what you can or cannot do in *my* candy shop." Just to punctuate his point, he winked and popped the ridiculous studs out of his dad's earlobes.

The last thing he needed right now was his dad looking through the books, especially with Colby standing right in earshot.

Dorian cracked his knuckles and closed his eyes. He was searching things out. A specialty of his dad's, and theoretically of his grandmother's as well. It had led to a lot of unwanted discovery when he was growing up. Lachlan could still remember the day he came home to find his box of underwear packaging, men's fitness magazines, and an illicitly acquired Playgirl he'd *suggested* the magazine stand owner sell him without checking his ID on the table, and his father on the other side, looking displeased.

But Lachlan wasn't a dumb, hormonal, untrained witch anymore. So he smiled and waited for the searching spell to inevitably fail. He maybe liked the scowl across his dad's face a little too much.

"We had an agreement, Lachlan."

"The courts would beg to differ. If you recall, we officially moved the business and the property into my name the last time you were up here. And because of that, I've taken measures in order to ensure that you don't have unfettered access to things that are mine."

"Laws are laws, and we are above them."

Lachlan rolled his eyes. "Sometimes I don't understand why Mom left you, you know? You sound so much like her sometimes, talking about how much better we are?" He shrugged. "Witches just have a little more knowledge in some areas than anyone else. It's no different than anything else." He glanced to the awkwardly shifting Colby again. "Again, there's a client present. So stop."

Dorian's eyes narrowed. "I knew this would end up happening. You've never been trustworthy."

That stung. Even if he didn't really care what his dad thought of him, he knew *exactly* what that meant. The comments about his trustworthiness had a long history between the two of them. And it had started with him hiding his box of jack off material, which his dad pretended was beyond the pale. It wasn't about him stealing the magazine, of course, or even having that kind of magazine at age fifteen. It was that it was a Play*girl*. It was that he kept the pictures of jacked dudes in nothing but their briefs. Liking boys? *That* apparently made him untrustworthy, since he couldn't so much as honor his father's wishes to continue on the family name.

But just before Lachlan threw down the shaker and started in on his dad—he had plenty of botanicals right in the kitchen and could throw a nasty pox together in a pinch, he was sure of it—Colby cleared his throat. "Mr. James. I really do need to talk with your son, now. And I happen to be heading back up to my parents' place on the cliff after I'm done here. They would hate to have me be late." He nodded firmly, stepping straight up to Dorian. "Magic is magic, and money is money, and influence comes from both, but I starkly believe that Grayson money can stand up to James magic in this situation. So are you a betting man?"

A mix of sensations burst through Lachlan as he stood there, watching this whole thing go down. Lachlan was defiant to his father, but the man was still intimidating. Yet there Colby stood, mouthing off to him, making vague threats. Lachlan's stomach dropped out, his mouth went dry, the back of his neck prickled, and a flush of warmth that wasn't entirely embarrassment, but not entirely something else, rushed from his chest and out to the very edges of his being.

Dorian stared him down a few seconds, then shrugged. "I'll be back." He never turned to look back at Lachlan, but it was eminently clear who he was talking to in this situation, in spite of his gaze still fixed firmly on Colby. "You know full well that given time and preparation, I'll be able to get what I want. I have reason to believe this shop is failing under your leadership. Law or no law, if the books play that out, I'm taking this place back until I can trust you with the family legacy."

He brushed past Colby, swinging the kitchen doors open with a sweep of his hand, and was gone, leaving just frazzled nerve endings and a looming specter of his return.

Once he was gone, Colby nodded, his shoulders relaxing. "You're right. He's...not the most pleasant man I've ever had to deal with."

"That's one way to put it." Lachlan let out what should have been a calming breath, but it felt like the extra room he made in his chest was just a nice breeding ground for more stress. He'd mouthed off. He'd somehow gotten Colby involved in his family conflict. Colby. The guy he'd hung out shirtless with, playing around, touching up on each other. Colby, a big meal ticket. Colby, a nice guy who really didn't deserve to be pulled into this crap. And what had all of that bought him? No more than a few days, because Dorian James could damn sure find those books if he really wanted to. And he could also damn sure take the shop back.

"Hey, why don't you take a break for a minute?" Colby's hand on his shoulder was the only thing that shocked Lachlan out of his spiraling thoughts. "You're really shaken by him, huh?"

And Lachlan couldn't very well lie, because the proof was plain in every cell of his body. "It's stupid, but just once I'd like to not be a disappointment to the man. Even if he is a dick. Just to *spite* him for all the years he's looked down on me. Really make something out of this shop that even he couldn't pull off." He took Colby's hand without even thinking about it, then pulled back when he realized what he'd done.

But Colby didn't let it go, clung onto it. "Is it inappropriate to ask for a look at your books? I'm a finance major after all."

Lachlan swallowed back a cry of anguish. "I'd really rather you didn't."

Colby lowered his glasses to the tip of his nose so he could look into Lachlan's eyes sans lenses. Those dark, demanding, encompassing eyes. "Your father and that underwear lady are the only other people I've seen in here since I started coming, and you have no end of time to work exclusively on my family's order." His words were definitely harsh, but his tone was understanding, warm, soft. And maybe most reassuringly, there was no sadness in the pits of those eyes. This wasn't *pity*. Just a statement of things Colby had seen over the last few days. "I already gathered that you might be struggling."

"Am I that bad at hiding it?"

"Only because I spend so much free time here instead of hanging out with my family. Although after meeting your dad, my overly doting parents don't seem that bad." He smiled just a touch. "That's only halfway a joke."

Lachlan offered him a slight smile in return. "I guess, if you already know what's up. In my defense, it's not *that* bad. I'm just consistently a little bit underwater." He didn't have anything currently on the burner that needed attending, so he waved Colby to walk behind him, back into the little magic room.

"This doesn't seem like the most inconspicuous place if you're trying to keep the books from your dad. Just saying."

"It's the safest place in the whole shop." He sighed, then screwed up his eyes like he had the morning of his and Colby's first meeting about the order, opening up spaces that weren't traditionally available. When he did so, he caught sight of the little accordion file keeper tucked between two tables that normally butted straight against each other.

What he didn't expect was a gasp when he reached for it.

Lachlan turned to see Colby slack-jawed and wide-eyed. "What?"

"You stuck your hand into the table legs. Didn't think to warn me?"

"Oh. I've never actually done it in front of anyone who didn't know what was up. Sorry." He pulled back and brought the accordion keeper with him. A thick black rectangle with a handle on the top. "Everything's in there." Lachlan's face burned at the thought of him seeing the paperwork. "Just, before you go through it, I already know the shop is costing the most and pulling the rest of it down, but I need the facilities here to run the rest of the business." He popped the buckle on the front and was met immediately with the scent of old, mostly dead herbs and spices. "There's a little cloth bag in the bottom of this. Don't take it out."

Colby nodded, but then looked straight back at Lachlan. "If it's super uncomfortable, I don't have to."

"I know. But I think you already know the worst of it." And genuinely, Lachlan smiled. "Not just anyone who can stand up to my dad like that. I sure as hell can't do it reliably. So maybe I need to be bold just this one time."

Yet as he turned away, headed back in to begin work on the next batch—he'd gone with the citrus and coffee infused caramels, the ones he'd started considering when he drank the latte and first smelled the bright, heady notes of Colby's cologne—his stomach still flip-flopped. He didn't talk finances with anyone, let alone a client. Let alone double a client studying finance. Let alone *triple* a client studying finance who'd invited him to a Halloween party so they could bone.

But maybe somehow even worse than that, he was nervous about what he was going to hear once Colby had looked at his books. How fucked was he really, when someone took a glance at his numbers *objectively*? Had he been fooling himself this entire time into thinking he could make this business work, make something happen left out on his own?

Or was he, as his father insisted, just a disappointing homosexual?

It took a solid hour before Colby made a reappearance, carrying a couple sheets of loose paper with him. In that time, Lachlan had started and finished the caramels, and gotten them wrapped up in the little bits of wax paper and placed into a sealed container to minimize the moisture absorption, the air contact, all that stuff. He was actually pouring some lollipops, and did his best not to panic when he saw Colby. "Well, dead on arrival?"

"I wouldn't say that." Colby pulled over a stool and sat well-enough away for food safety, but close enough for easy conversation. "You're completely right that you can't get rid of the shop. I did just a brief number crunch, nothing too official, to see what it would take to meet standards without the shop's kitchen, and it's not tenable."

"Well at least I'm not an idiot."

"You're not an idiot at all. That's also not what I was looking for." He sighed, and he smiled. "I actually do have a suggestion on how you could make some changes in order to make the business a little more viable."

"Already?"

He nodded. "I mean, I have two, but I have a feeling you'll turn me down as an angel investor."

"I would."

"Exactly. But I think the biggest draw you have on this is simply that...you're a candy shop. Just a candy shop. I'm not a marketing genius or anything, but I can tell that you lose a lot of money you don't have to because of your stock."

"My stock?"

"You don't sell day-in, day-out. I think you'd do better if you were completely boutique, made-to-order. You wouldn't need to keep the shop front open every day, you wouldn't need to keep jars and jars of candy that you eventually throw out, and you'd be able to create the proper air of exclusivity to coincide with the skill you have in confectionery."

"Well that would be great, but is that really going to save me enough money?"

"Save money, probably not. There's a bit of a gamble involved in the whole situation, but I believe it would work out." He handed over one of the sheets of paper. "With the turnover on your stock, you're throwing out a decent amount every month. And you can see the general estimates on the power you'd be able to save jut by not having to keep a shop front. You'd also save time, you'd save stress, which is a big deal, and…well, I can't predict the future. That's more in your wheelhouse than mine. But I think it would be worth attempting to just do made-to-order, boutique candy instead of regular hours, normal stock wrangling, all that."

Lachlan sat with the idea. He really did. It was a nice idea, if he could make it work. He was underwater consistently. But what if closing down the shop front completely killed the business? The numbers on the sheet didn't suggest he could suddenly make up the differences. There was no magic bullet. *And I should know about magic bullets.*

"It's your business, obviously. But maybe this party will be a good test?" Colby nodded matter of factly. "I figure, the party's going to expose your work to the sort of clientele you deserve to have patronizing you. And since you already have online ordering set up…"

He really does want to help. Even if the thought of any of this clenched cold and iron around Lachlan's belly, he knew Colby really thought this was a good, solid decision. He wasn't attempting to lead Lachlan astray. *And something has to change, here.* "I guess we'll see how the party goes."

"Good." Colby smiled, then stood. "And then we can celebrate, if you're still interested in that part of the offer."

"If anything's changed, that's not it." In fact, looking at

Colby, taking in the sharp slopes of his cheek bones and the softness and shininess of his hair, the rest of the worry began to ease. Just a bit. Enough for him to breathe. Enough he could consider what was next to make.

Colby nodded, and then he approached. "Could I make one request of payment for my grueling service to your finances, then?"

"I suppose." Colby was so close the whole world smelled of oranges and brightness, and his skin seemed endless and warm and inviting as Lachlan remembered finding that tiny pulse of life with his lips in the living room.

Colby leaned in close and whispered in his ear, even though they were totally in private. "I'm going to swear again, but I want you to squeeze my ass."

"Oh, how will I ever survive such a hideous invoice request?" Lachlan reached around, running his hand down the soft material of the sweater. Colby's breath hitched in his ear as he passed his fingers below the waist of the jeans. He tightened his fingers around a taut, firm globe of muscle, and a twinge passed down his spine and into his crotch, begging him to go further and filling his mind with memories of soft skin and lightly defined pecs, and fantasies of a lavish cliff-side home filled with people who had no idea what a candy-maker and a finance student were doing in the bedroom up above them.

"Thanks." Colby pulled away, and his blush was as all-encompassing as Lachlan had ever seen it. "I think that should tide me over for now."

"Well, I have more if you think you undercharged at any point." This was nice. This was the lack of stress and worry that Colby had been telling him was important. Madcap, sensual, sheer sensation and infatuation carrying them forward through this intense tango.

"I'm going to head out. My cousin won't be coming in for

the party after all, so I have to pick up her order at Mendelssohn's Hardware."

"Wow, hardware store? You really go all out for this thing, don't you?"

"I guess you'll definitely have to make an appearance in order to find out." Colby snapped his fingers. "Right. Your invitation. When your dad showed up, I got distracted." He fished into his back pocket—on the cheek Lachlan *hadn't* felt up—and produced a thick sheaf of paper, folded and sealed with actual wax. "That will get you in the door."

"Seriously. All out."

Colby shrugged. "Halloween is but once per year. Why not do things properly?" He moved toward the double doors. "I will see you later."

And he was gone. Lachlan sighed, running his fingers over the invitation, still sealed, and running his eyes back over the numbers Colby had scratched out on those papers. *A boutique candy shop, huh?* The thought still curdled his stomach, but he squeezed his eyes shut. The only way to know how it would go was to actually take a swing.

The party with the rich folks would be his test. And if he failed that test...well, Lachlan sincerely hoped he wouldn't, because it felt like he had few other options.

After wrapping up his work, Lachlan headed home. And on his front porch sat a small package wrapped in bright green fabric. He knew better than to touch it, at least, but when he even got close to it, the fabric flapped open, and a voice emanated from within. Dorian James's voice. "You won't make a mockery of this family. I'm not leaving peacefully."

And inside the box, after the voice had faded, was a distinctive mark, one Lachlan new because his father used it for those who angered him. A lot of people angered him. It was a single dried lily with a silver bell tied around the stem. Lachlan's gut dropped through his feet, and he immediately rushed inside, careful not to disturb the box on his way.

Had things fallen *this* far off? The lily, the flower of the dead, and a bell. The silver bell was a common missive of aggression between witches, would make them known with a single ring, no matter how hard they tried to hide. But the lily, questionably effective as it may have been, was meant to signal psychopomps. Spirits who would guide the dead to the underworld. If they showed up and there was no one to take, as there wouldn't be here, then they wouldn't be happy campers.

Again, Lachlan was uncertain how well this actually functioned, or if his father had even completed the work. He'd always hidden the final steps of that spell from Lachlan. But he wouldn't be taking chances. He grabbed the salt from up above the microwave, a blue candle, and the little jar of various dead insects he kept on hand for strange magics just like this. Then he lit the candle, blue to repel evil, surrounded the lily with salt, and finally laid the bug inside the circle of salt. Only then could he confidently reach in and remove the bell, careful to hold the clapper silent.

After that, he burned the lily in the flame of the candle, chucked the box and the bell away, and headed in. He needed to talk to someone who could understand, who would listen to him. He needed to find the phone number for Shady Grove Retirement Village.

ot working on the order, or the couple online shipments he had in the works, was a little bit of a hindrance, but if his dad was actually threatening him, there was only one place, one person, Lachlan could hope would help him out.

Shady Grove was the only actual retirement community in Cape Elizabeth proper, and it was a spendy one. The unspoken, but well-known, family secret was that Martha James was paid for entirely by a series of clients she'd done some hefty magic for over the years. Once, she'd let slip to Lachlan that one of her clients had set her up with a percentage of his trust, so that even after his death, she'd be taken care of. "That's what fixing powerful men's dicks can get you."

And Lachlan had to smile at the memory, because while he hadn't yet gotten to fix any *powerful* men's dicks, he did know you could upcharge significantly if you could get a guy raging boners again. Too many guys put too much stock in their ability to get it up, and they'd happily shell out the big bucks to return to their "prime."

Lachlan walked through the beige entryway into the

mauve interior. The man at the front desk locked eyes with him. "Can I help you?"

"I'm here to see Martha James. I'm her grandson."

"Oh, yes, she's been expecting you."

Considering Lachlan hadn't called in before coming over, he should have been surprised. But he wasn't. Grandma was always particularly gifted in matters of clairvoyance and clairaudience.

The man led him back to room 121 and knocked for him. "Martha. You have a visitor."

The door swung open. "Lachlan." Martha James was, again, very similar in appearance to him and his father. More obvious in her older pictures, showing her statuesque form, her handsome jawline, and the signature dark hair. Now in her late seventies—she never revealed her age beyond that level of specificity—she was left with only a small shock of that ebony hair left in a sea of gentle white waves. She still wore large hoop earrings every day, her fingers bedecked in rings. Today, she wore a white, empire-waisted dress covered in pale pink roses, and as proof that she'd been expecting company, she had far too much rouge on her cheeks. Her signature look even in old photographs.

He stepped in and hugged her tight, and she returned a shockingly strong squeeze. The attendant walked away, and with a wink, Martha shut the door behind him.

She lowered herself into a wicker chair, and Lachlan took the one opposite her. "Hey, Gram."

"I'd like to think it's just my grandson visiting me, but you have an aura of dark thoughts around you. And you visited me at the beginning of the month already."

"That obvious?"

"Not worth trying to slip things past an old witch." She sighed, then fixed warm brown eyes on him. "What's bad enough that you felt the need to come see me."

"Well, if you didn't know, your son's back in town."

"Oh, if he's my son instead of your dad, things must be bad."

"Well, he's a dick. No fault of your own, I'm sure."

"Maybe some fault of my own. I raised him." She smiled and sighed. "But I won't take more than ten percent credit for that part of his personality."

"Anyway, he wanted to see the books for *my* shop. You know, the one he signed over entirely to me a year ago? Well I said no, he tried to find them, I already had them protected because I know him. When I got home after work, he'd left me a package. Told me he'd get his way. And in the box was a lily and bell."

The corners of her mouth turned down. "Lily and bell. Well, I can agree that he's a bit of a dick, but I suppose it's time you know the truth about that spell. It's useless."

It took Lachlan a minute to recover from that casually tossed grenade. "What?"

"Honestly, I thought you knew. It's a scare tactic. We've always kept it close to the vest, shared out enough information about it that people knew what it was theoretically supposed to do, but that's it."

"But a bunch of people he sent them to were actually bothered. They had terrible luck, or they got sick, or they suddenly lost money."

"Well, people see the lily and bell, know who it's from, know what it's supposed to do, and they don't check for a small bit of the pox, or something to give them a heavy period, or whatever else seemed useful at the time."

"Dad gave someone a heavier period?"

"No, I did. In high school. But in my defense, Kathleen Bollier was a haughty bitch. She's lucky I didn't just make her late. God knows she was sleeping with Jack enough it would have given her a good scare."

"Remind me not to get on your bad side."

"Oh, you could never get on my bad side, sweetie." She

reached across and patted him on the cheek. "Well, it isn't a glowing review of him as a father if he's sending you the lily and bell just to scare you, I'll say that. But he's not trying to actually ruin your life."

"Yet."

"The business. Still struggling along?"

Gram was one of the few who knew the ins and outs of Lachlan's business, so he could at least talk to her. "It got a little better recently. I'm doing the whole candy order for the Grayson Halloween party. Don't know if it's going to do much for me from there, but it's a nice boost to my income."

"You're hoping it has long term effects?"

"I was…invited by the Grayson's son. And he thinks if I'm there with the candy, I'll be able to pull in a bunch of rich clients." His tongue and lips kept going, finally able to talk about this whole thing with someone he trusted. Because he certainly couldn't trust himself to be objective or clear-headed about *anything* to do with Colby. "He's also a finance major, and I let him look at the books, and he thinks I'd be better off doing a boutique, made-to-order setup with the shop."

"The same way you do magic, then."

That stopped Lachlan for a few seconds while he thought about it. "I suppose, yeah."

"You've said the magic tends to be more profitable, right? You can charge whatever you need to because it's custom, basically." She began to smile as she spoke. "Honestly, it sounds like a decent idea, if I may be so bold as to make a suggestion about your own shop."

"Well it's your shop, too."

She shook her head. "We have to be fair about this. If you're the owner, so your father has no say, then I certainly have no say. I passed it to him over twenty years ago, divested myself of the whole thing. It's *your* shop, even if it's the family name."

And Lachlan felt an overwhelming sense of calm wash

through him. Visceral enough he had to ask, "Are you magicking me right now?"

"No." She shook her head, brows knitting in the center. "Are you feeling all right? I have a bottle of seawater on hand for just such a situation."

"No. It's fine. Just wanted to make sure." Something about hearing all that from an outside point of view, it truly gave him solid footing again. He wasn't walking into this like some overly infatuated fool. Running the shop that way made sense according to someone else, too. Someone with experience running a candy/magic shop, nonetheless. Not a terribly common opinion that could just be harvested off some internet forum. "If I do that, Dad's going to have a coronary."

"Too bad he has no actual recourse to control that shop then, isn't it? He'll just have to have it in Bora Bora."

"You're cold, Gram."

"He can take care of himself. And if he wants to come after my grandbaby like that, he's going to have to cope with me." She twisted her fingers, circled her wrists, rings gleaming in the gentle lamplight from her bedside table. "I may be in a retirement home, but I happen to have some of his baby teeth on hand. I can make him shit himself for a week if necessary."

"You don't have to do that."

She chuckled dryly. "I'm hoping I don't. But I'm in your corner if necessary. Really, it would be simple." She leaned back into her chair and grabbed the teacup from her side table. "So this Grayson. You make a habit of sharing your finances with clients?"

"I do when they're cute."

A smile spread across her face, cutting the wrinkles around her mouth deeper as her eyes sparkled with light. "I can't say I'm surprised. I may have checked in on you one night. Did you try to give him a hickey in your living room?"

And yeah, *that* was a particular experience he didn't need

to go into with his grandma. "I don't think our relationship is at the point where we need to go into detail about that, Gram. But we're...I don't know what we're doing, exactly, but there's this magnetism between us both."

She nodded. "If I can make a suggestion that might seem radical to you? Try just being happy for a little while. If playing weird sex games with the rich boy makes you happy, then I'll print you out directions to the kink store myself."

"*Gram.*"

She chuckled lightly. "I'm kidding. I doubt you need directions."

And he couldn't help but laugh, and enjoy the time with his grandmother, and bask in the strange sense of reassurance he'd somehow stumbled his way into.

And yeah, even if his dad was a dick for trying to fucking intimidate him, he had to admit he was happy that the lily and bell was bullshit, that his dad wasn't actually trying to harm him.

But like hell he was giving up the shop, or the books. *Now just to see how this party goes.*

CHAPTER EIGHT

The next few days were a blur of activity. Whether by pure luck, universal meddling, or his groundwork finally paying off, he'd gotten several large online orders, including three pounds of honeycomb that nearly flooded out of the pot when he added the baking soda. He only actually kept things under control with a swirl of his will, forcing the bubbling molten sugar to behave until it calmed and sank back into the pot.

Suddenly, it was Halloween, and as he rose, he realized he didn't know what kind of party he was actually meant to prepare for. But luckily, as he expected, Colby arrived at the shop, still bundled up, but with coffee in hand, which gave him a chance to go straight for the heart of the matter. "Is this a costume party?"

"Costume, no. But you're likely to see some outlandish dress choices. No pirates or sexy nurses, though."

Well, that was all right. Lachlan had *some* finer clothes. Not to the level of the folks who were going to be in attendance, but he'd had his year or two of living his best gay young witch fantasy. *Maybe I'll go for the metallic paisley blazer.*

He couldn't think of anything more *outlandish* hanging out in his closet at the moment.

This time, Lachlan headed to the door and flipped the lock over, took the OPEN sign off the door. Then he just headed into the kitchen sans explanation.

Colby definitely noticed. "A candy shop not open on Halloween?"

"I'll open if someone shows up looking for candy." Lachlan smiled as he tied the apron around his waist. "I think I'd like to give this boutique thing a try."

"Really?"

"What do I have to lose at this point? You've seen my numbers. If nothing changes, I can keep this place open, what, another six months? Maybe a year?"

"That's selling yourself a bit short, I think."

"Still." It twisted Lachlan's stomach, but not as much as the overwhelming, existential spread of inactivity he'd been living with for the better part of the last year. "It's sink or swim time, and like you said, I should give this party a chance to actually work for me."

"Well, it can start working for you now." He dug into his pocket, pulling out his wallet, and he produced a stack of bills. "I'm giving you a tip because you've done so much extra work and gotten me out of the house during this time of family togetherness, and I don't want to hear anything about it."

Lachlan took the money and gave it a quick count. "This is five hundred dollars."

"Yes."

"When we talked about it, we agreed on three hundred."

"Yes. I don't want to hear about it."

"You're going to hear about it. You've given me a sixty-seven percent tip."

"It's because I knew you wouldn't take a hundred percent tip."

"If this is a subtle way to make sure that I'm going to fool around with you tonight, I'm a lot cheaper than two hundred bucks a night."

"I'm not paying you for sex. I'm paying you for candy making. Hell, you could rebuff me completely tonight if you wanted."

Lachlan looked him up and down, took in the tight-fitting blue top, the acid-washed jeans, the hint of smile tugging up the corners of his lips. "Honestly? I don't think I could." He'd been longing for Colby, had even restrained himself from *handling things* on his own the last few days, just to make sure everything would be satisfying.

Colby grinned broad at him. "I can't say I'm disappointed." Then he clapped his hands together. "So can I help with anything? Last touches? Wrapping tiny candies until my fingers bleed?"

"Really trying to avoid the family?"

"Not so much. I just like spending time with you."

"Because I'm interesting?"

"Well, yes. But also, if you're the sort of person willing to make a big jump in your only source of income, I think I'd like to get my hands dirty to help you out."

"Well, not too dirty." *He wants to help.* And honestly, not many people spoke so highly of Lachlan. None of his one or two previous long-terms. *Not that we're long-term.* "How do you feel about cutting marshmallows?"

"Isn't that a bit of a big job for an intern?"

"I think you can manage it." He gestured Colby over. "Come on." The three pans of drying marshmallows were laid out on one of the stainless steel prep benches. He grabbed a knife and a prep tray, then brought over the powdered sugar. "It's not too hard. You just need to be liberal with the powdered sugar so nothing sticks." He yanked on the parchment paper and removed one of the solid blocks of fluffy white marshmallow. He flipped it over and peeled everything free. "One pan should make ninety-six marshmallows." He coated the edge of the knife in powdered sugar. Colby cringed as his fingers got too close to the blade, but Lachlan just kept moving, slicing rows of marshmallow in clean, even movements. Eleven cuts, twelve strips. Then he quickly cut them into cubes and transferred them handful by handful into the tray of powdered sugar. "Then you just toss them and you're good to go."

"Maybe I should stick to finance."

Lachlan chuckled and laid the knife aside. "Do we need to Patrick Swayze this?" But Lachlan didn't wait for an answer, moved deftly behind Colby. It worked well because Lachlan had a few inches on him…but not so many he couldn't rub up against Colby's ass just a little bit. "Okay, so just do what I did, and I'll correct you if necessary."

"Okay." Colby's voice was high, tight as it slipped out. He cleared his throat before speaking again. "You're trying to get me to hook up early?"

"Nope. I'm just helping you cut marshmallows." He shifted a little bit, was already hardening in his jeans. "If you want me to stop helping, I can."

"No." Colby shot it out quickly, slightly frantic. "I'm…so I flip them out first, right?"

"Right." Lachlan watched him remove the marshmallow block and lay it out in the already existing puddle of powdered sugar. "Then you want to cut it into twelve by eight. Ninety-six. If they're a little uneven, it's fine. We just point out that they're handmade."

He nodded, grabbed the knife, and laid it into the powdered sugar, one side, then the other. When he moved to make the first cut, Lachlan gently cupped his fingers around Colby's hand, pressed forearm to forearm, and guided him toward the center. "When you're not familiar with it, it's easier to cut it in half, then half, then half." Did Lachlan *maybe* lower his voice into a husky whisper, lean his mouth in so he was speaking straight into Colby's ear?

Possibly.

Colby moved jerkily, but Lachlan took control, shifting him smoothly, letting the knife do the work as he absorbed the bright scent of citrus that lingered on the back of Colby's neck, behind his ears.

It took longer than was strictly necessary to cut, but they soon had marshmallows. Lachlan moved away from Colby, sliding around so he could face him, and grabbed one of the corner marshmallows. They always wound up a little bit deformed, so no one would miss just one. He held it out and nodded to Colby. "Try it."

A tiny jerk of hesitation, a hitch in Colby's breath. He raised a shivery hand and pressed his glasses back up the bridge of his nose, then he finally leaned in, parting his lips, and took the marshmallow between neat white teeth. His lips brushed soft and supple against Lachlan's fingertips.

Colby chewed a few seconds, the muscles of his jaw moving visibly this close up. Then his eyes widened. "What is that flavor?"

"Passion fruit. You didn't get a chance to test this one, but I thought you might like it."

"I do. I just don't think I've had passion fruit before." He swallowed what remained and smiled. "It's really good. Not what I was expecting from a marshmallow, but it really works. It's so soft and plush, and then it's really tropical and overwhelming. It's *really* good."

Lachlan smiled. "Well, glad to have the seal of approval." He took one himself, another corner piece, and popped it into his mouth. The juxtaposition was lovely, a lot less jarring than it had been during his very first test batch. He'd used too much of the passion fruit extract, plus had also miscalculated the amount of gelatin he needed, so they were too stiff and too citric and just wrong. Now, with a softer texture and a lighter touch, they became almost like a foam. A cloud of passion fruit and sugar. "That is good, you're right."

"I mean it. You'll be lucky if those make it out of here anywhere outside of my belly."

In response, Lachlan sparked off his fingers, letting them issue a little smoke. "It may be your order, but you paid me to bring it to the party."

Colby held up his hands in surrender. "Do your fingers actually get warm when you do that?"

Lachlan touched them to his cheek. "Warm?"

"Yeah, I'd say so." Without warning, Colby kissed those fingertips. "I probably can't stay all day. But, um…ribbed for his pleasure?"

Lachlan smiled in spite of the heat cruising up his neck and face and into his ears. "That's fine with me. Uh, dealer's choice."

"Cool." Lachlan didn't miss the rosiness in Colby's cheeks, but said nothing, just took a last look at his ass as Colby walked out the kitchen doors. His mind went to impure places.

And pretty soon, if all played out well, his body would also go to those same impure places.

⊱⊰

The Grayson house stood atop a cliff, overlooking what was now a roiling, gray cauldron. Haze shivered over the surface of the water as Lachlan hauled tubs full of candy up to the front steps. All in all, for the kind of money Colby had paid him, he had three big plastic containers filled with confections, plus a smaller box that contained some of the more fragile candies, as well as the labels he'd whipped together. His handwriting was shit, but a little hint of magic not only made his penmanship beautiful, but it made the ink shimmer just slightly, a minor iridescence that looked especially lovely against the ivory parchment. Or at least he thought so.

The front steps of the the three story manor had been decked out with all manner of Halloween-appropriate decorations. None of the admittedly tacky bats and pumpkins and spiders of construction paper that Lachlan had up around the shop front. Instead, the two story columns supporting the portico had been wrapped in spirals of taut, black and purple butcher paper, applied without a single bubble or ripple in sight. Hanging from that portico were old-fashioned string lights, the kind with large, round bulbs that cast a warm glow, but through red mesh of some sort that gave the whole space an eerie tint. Of course, the very nature of the house, an old, Queen Anne style building in charcoal gray, lent itself well to the slightly unsettling feeling of the whole thing.

Though in the end, Lachlan was pretty sure a lot of his own unease was how little he felt like he belonged, and how much he felt his future riding on this party.

He grabbed the doorknocker, a heavy brass ring hanging from the mouth of a skull that Lachlan had a suspicion was added specifically for Halloween, and tapped it twice against the wood. After a few moments, the large door swung open, revealing a woman, Korean if he were to guess, like he had with Colby. Her hair was pure ebony, slicked and shined and falling in pin curls to frame a round face. She came up only to Lachlan's collarbone, even in three-inch heels, and the bejeweled frames of her glasses reflected the gleaming red from outside. "Can I help you?"

Lachlan reached into the inner pocket of his jacket and presented the invitation. "Colby Grayson invited me. And also, I'm here with all the candy."

Her face broke into a smile, and she gave the same sort of half-chuckle that Colby did. "Well come in." She slipped around him, surprisingly nimble in spite of her footwear, and grabbed one of the large bins. "We'll drop these in the ball-room and you can get them all set up."

"I can really haul them myself."

"Yes, but I can only sit around drinking Merlot so long. It's good to get my body moving." She clipped through the entry-way, shoes clacking, and the beaded fringe of her cocktail dress shifted side to side with each step, leaving a wake of rustling behind her. "You've saved me from being too drunk to socialize when the other guests arrive."

Together, they got all the confections moved into…well, Lachlan had never seen a ballroom outside of a hotel, and certainly not one actually outfitted for a proper party, but this was almost certainly a ballroom. About twenty tables filled the massive space, by itself two stories high. More of those old-fashioned string lights adorned the walls and ceiling, thought without the red mesh. It simply made the space feel warm and inviting. The floor was marble, polished to a near mirror finish, and the tablecloths were all a deep plum color, reminiscent of the purple on the columns outside. Fireplaces on either side crackled with gentle flames, and a chandelier of a hundred or more glass tubes hung in the center, filling in the rest of the illumination.

However, aside from the two of them, the whole space was entirely devoid of people. Lachlan flashed to thoughts of a party so exclusive no one actually made an appearance. *Of course, it doesn't help that I came half an hour early to set up.*

"So the candy can go right here." She gestured to a trio of tables left empty next to the massive pair of punch crystal punch bowls. "Oh, I never introduced myself." She daintily extended a hand. "Joann Grayson."

"Lachlan James."

"Yes, I've heard a lot about you from Colby." She picked up a wine glass that had apparently been left behind next to the punch. "He tells me you're quite the confectioner. And he also mentioned you have a *side* business."

"A side business?"

She lowered her voice even though they were alone. "You do magic for people?"

Well, not like I'm in the habit of hiding that. It took him by surprise that Colby would mention it, but also that she would apparently believe him. "Off and on. As the money dictates."

And like he'd seen the half-chuckle before, he got to hear where Colby got that rare, full laugh. It rocked from her the same way it did from him, out of her belly and up past heavily arched lips. "That is splendid. I don't suppose you could make...well, I don't know what you'd have to make, but my cousin, she's married to a piece of...can I swear?"

One more thing he gets from her. "Yes."

"She's married to a piece of shit. He's not hitting her, but he's essentially living off her, no interest in taking care of himself or contributing. He threatens suicide every time she suggests she might leave."

"I can make you a leech remover." He winked. "It'll be a hundred bucks, but I can do it."

"I'd happily pay more than that if it got her into a healthier situation." She sighed. "Sorry for that business talk. I promise that's the only time I'll bring it up, but I can't speak for anyone else." She hovered nearby with her wine as he removed lids from the crates. "Is there something I can do to help?"

He went for the one bin with the heavier wares and pulled out his forest green boxes. "Are these going to completely be beyond the pale for presentation?"

She eyed them for a few seconds, then shrugged. "I don't see any issue with it."

Lachlan nodded and began to set the candies out. Joann, without waiting for him to say yea or nay, began unboxing things, and he couldn't help smiling as she gasped at the sight of various different confections, commenting as she handed him each one to be laid out.

"Ooh, this is that brittle. Colby brought it home a week ago. I made sure to request that was here."

"Help yourself."

"I will." And she grabbed one of the larger shards before passing over the rest. "It really is delightful."

"Joann, do we have enough hors d'oeuvres? Do we need to put more out?" A high tenor careened through the space, echoing lightly in the cavernous ballroom. Soon behind it came a tall, round-bodied Black man, wearing a full three-piece suit, plum to match the tablecloths, and with a brilliantly white tie. His gaze flicked to Joann, then to Lachlan. "Oh, I see. I wasn't aware you were in the midst of an amorous tryst. I'll come back in ten minutes?"

"Please. A woman like me needs longer than ten minutes. Besides, I wouldn't dream of robbing him away from Colby."

That made Lachlan almost drop a box of green apple lollipops on the floor. "What?"

"Oh, we shouldn't be aware that our son is infatuated with the candymaking magic boy he spends all his time with and won't stop talking about?" Her eyes gleamed, dark, but not in the drawing, demanding way that Colby's were. "He's not been the most subtle."

"Oh, so this is Lachlan." He marched up, hand held out. "Roland Grayson."

"Lachlan. James." He hated that he was staring, but he was.

And apparently Roland noticed. "He's my stepson." Roland gestured from his head down. "Trust me, these genes are robust and would have made him ten times as handsome as he already is."

"Right. Sorry."

"Don't be sorry. You brought me candy. No one brings me candy. Not even my loving wife."

"Careful." She pinched one of his cheeks. "I might still

find time for a *real* amorous tryst if you don't watch your step."

He took her hand and kissed the back of it. "I'm sure Colby will be down soon. Is there anything we can do to help you set up?" He reached over and took the edge of Lachlan's paisley jacket between his thumb and forefinger. "I like this quite a bit, by the way."

Compared to the slightly timid nature of Colby, his parents were extra extra. Lachlan grinned to himself, still setting out boxes of candy, as he imagined a ten year old Colby trying and failing to disappear from simply embarrassing levels of affection trained on him by doting parents.

And as he crossed into Lachlan's mind, he made an appearance, sweeping down the stairs just behind Roland. And Lachlan was taken slightly aback. It was the first time he'd seen him out of some combination of a sweater and jeans. But now, he wore a shimmery, midnight blue jacket over a white button down, and dress pants that were equally white. Everything was fitted, and for the first time, Lachlan really got that Colby had money, came from money. That kind of clothing, it was definitely custom-tailored. Off-the-rack clothes didn't hug to curves, pinch in the waist, outline the form in such a precise way. He'd slicked his hair all the way back from his forehead, behind his ears.

He made a beeline straight for Lachlan, and smiled gently. "You made it."

"You paid me way too much money. Of course I made it." He turned his attention away from Colby in order to keep from blushing or staring or drooling or anything else. Plus he still had candy that needed putting out, anyway, although at the moment, the space was currently about half-filled with green boxes of various confections. When he got to the marshmallows, he was taken back to that moment in the kitchen, the feel of their forearms pressed against each other, the softness of Colby's lips against his fingertips. He felt an unwelcome growth in his crotch, especially given that his slacks for this outfit were a lot more form-fitting than he was used to. No comfy cotton here.

Before he could get everything laid out, Colby swung around and grabbed one of the boxes of marshmallows— almost three-hundred marshmallows didn't fit in one little green box—and presented it out to his parents. "You have to try these things. I was completely taken aback."

They both went in greedily and took heavy bites of the marshmallow, and Lachlan allowed himself to shift just a little bit to the side so he could take in their reactions without being too obvious.

"Passion fruit." Roland's face broke open into a smile, and he happily took the rest of it back. "I could injure myself eating those."

"I don't think I've had something that tastes this much like passion fruit since…well, since the last time I had actual passion fruit." Joann took another dainty bite of the marsh-mallow. "Did you pay him enough?"

"He paid me plenty." Lachlan glanced over at Colby. "Can you leave some of the marshmallows, and also start putting out the cards in front of the boxes? You know what basically everything here is by now."

Colby nodded and moved in. Between the pair of them, they made fairly quick work of the rest of the setup, and still before guests had arrived. And by stroke of luck, Joann and Roland had both walked away, leaving the pair of them alone.

Colby sighed as he shuffled through the cards, placing them in front of the appropriate boxes when he came across something that matched. "So, I figure I should let you know… I went ribbed. Since I like ribbed."

It took Lachlan a moment to catch up. "Oh. Good." An icy shiver crawled from the base of Lachlan's spine, nerves that met the gush of warmth that floated down from his head as he considered grasping Colby's waist, pulling him closer, listening to him gasp and ask for more. "I'm good with that plan." He cleared his throat to make it sound a little less *needy*. "Do we have a signal for when we should slip out?"

"Well, I was thinking of something subtle. I would come over and ask you to help me with something upstairs. But if you want, we can have a complex series of hand signals." He grinned lightly at Lachlan. "No need to overthink. Just breathe. Have some punch. I guarantee it's got enough rum in it to relax you."

Lachlan didn't even need convincing. A drink or three would relax him, not just for the tittering excitement over his coming time with Colby, but with the guests who would be hitting any time now. So once they got the candy set out, the bins tucked back into a closet just off the ballroom, and Lachlan's car parked somewhere other than directly in front of the door, he came in for a hearty swig of the punch. It tasted of rum, that much was for certain, and citrus and berries, and something in it fizzed against his tongue.

Then came a knock at the door, and Lachlan tensed. This was it. His potential "boutique clientele" would be walking through that door, filling this Queen Anne manor, examining his work right in front of him.

He poured another drink as the first couple was seen inside.

CHAPTER NINE

*L*achlan had never been to quite such a party as this. It certainly wasn't what he thought of when "Halloween party" passed through his mind. For the first hour or so, aside from the decor and the presence of entirely too much candy for a room full of adults, there was nothing that spoke to this being anything but a charity event for some generic politician. People from all across the country had come in for the event, and even some Canadians, since they were so close to the border as it was.

Lachlan did his best not to hover too close to the candy table, but stayed near enough that he could agonize every time someone tried something. Not one complaint. Several people took from his stack of business cards,and he even got accosted a few times at the party, people looking to talk to him directly. Apparently Colby or his parents had sent them his way. In that first hour alone, Lachlan put together two tastings and consultations over the next three days, and had several hastily texted orders on his phone for various confections that he'd brought to the house.

As the party continued on, the Halloween aesthetic became clearer and clearer. That was the effect of liquor, though. Halloween was largely a holiday of childlike glee, and the only thing that would truly make this many upper crust adults sink into that was liberal application of booze. It also helped that, at some point, the soundtrack for the evening shifted from vaguely dark classical music like Totentanz, Toccata and Fugue, and Holst's Neptune, and moved into heavy metal and classic rock strewn with mentions of demons and devils and the undead. That sort of music, maybe as much as the heavily spiked punch that kept getting mysteriously replenished, helped in uncinching some cummerbunds and removing some hair pins.

The gentle murmur of alcohol and screaming guitar also got to Lachlan. He found Colby mingling, and as soon as they were together, he murmured. "Watch this." He focused on the gentle lights up above and made them flicker. First subtly, then more rapidly, out of sync with the driving bass drum beat of the current song. People gasped and muttered, but when he released it, they seemed fine again.

"Big stuff."

"Little stuff. But I don't get to show it off very often, so let me have it?" He nuzzled against Colby and sighed. "Thank you. I'm getting the distinct impression that I can *maybe* pull off this custom ordering plan after all."

"Really? You've already gotten that much interest?"

"I've already gotten five orders and two people who want to come into the shop before they leave Cape Elizabeth. Plus your mom wants me to work up some kind of magic for her."

"My mom's buying magic off of you?" Colby's brows knitted. "It doesn't involve boiling my dad's underwear does it? Actually, I don't want to know."

"It's not about your parents. They're *ridiculously* in love with each other." At the moment, they were sharing a marshmallow, mouth to mouth. "But I'm a professional, so I can't say what it's about."

Colby nodded. "Need me to give you the good gossip on your potential clients?"

Lachlan considered it, but shook his head. "You gave me a platform to work from. I want to sink or swim on my own from here."

"I'm sure you'll swim just fine. If I'd known about your place, I'd have been stopping by every time I was in twon."

A tiny pang of sadness froze through Lachlan's midsection at the reminder that Colby *didn't* live here. He was leaving after this party. But he brushed it aside into a place he could drown out with rum.

"So I figure that now might be a decent time to slip upstairs." Colby's face was as crimson as the pumpkin seed brittle, but he held stiff, unwavering eye contact. "I know myself, and if I stay down here longer, I'll drink a lot more of that punch, and then I can't promise I'll be *functional* when we do go upstairs."

"Well, then lead the way." Lachlan tossed back what remained of his punch, linked arms with Colby, and they headed up, Lachlan dropping his empty glass on a nearby table filled with other empty punch glasses, plates, all sorts of things that needed addressing. No one seemed to be paying any attention to them, even though they were the only two people walking up the steps. And hell, even the *stairs* in this place took Lachlan a little bit by surprise. Fine finials and railing of dark wood, plush carpet that even felt soft through the soles of Lachlan's shoes. And as they reached the second floor landing, the separation between the floors was apparently enough that the music and the chatter faded into a gentle murmur from down below, a gentle thrum through his feet.

Colby led him through a dark wood door carved with many flowers, a smooth brass handle that moved smoothly, clicked ever so gently. The room inside was *intense*. Not at all what Lachlan would have expected from the rest of the house. Which wasn't entirely fair. Of course Colby's room wouldn't have to look like the rest of the Queen Anne home. The walls were a steely gray, with a chair rail of navy banded out by matching molding. The furniture was all in wood, stained an equally pale gray. From the dresser to the hamper to the massive bed frame that took up the majority of the floor space in the room. A king, if Lachlan was at all capable of estimating bed sizes, and decked out in deep navy bedding and pillows.

Colby closed the door behind him and crossed over to the nightstand. He pressed in on the drawer front and it popped open. He reached in and retrieved a too large box of condoms —considering this was one night, Lachlan had expected, like, a three pack, not the economy size—and a small, purple bottle of lube. "I hope this stuff is okay." He was still blushing hard, but *still* making eye contact with those dark, demanding eyes of his.

"It's fine." Lachlan smiled, and he knew Colby was nervous, and he had just enough rum in his system that he was warm and already kind of wanted to take off his clothes. So he slipped out of his shoes, and out of his jacket, and undid the buttons of his shirt until he could pull that off over his head. He didn't take care with it, just tossed it aside to be retrieved later. "Does that make it easier?"

Colby gave his little half-chuckle. "It helps."

He started to take off his jacket, but Lachlan stepped up and grabbed it, stripping it away from his shoulders, down his arms. The material was soft beneath his touch. "How about you let me do the work right now?"

Colby didn't argue, and Lachlan relished the feel of each garment beneath his touch, the way the fabric was warm from Colby's body, scented with wine and rum and citrus and sugar, though some of that well could have been his breath, standing so close they could only breathe each other's air.

As he stripped Colby out of his shirt, his fingers glanced

over the lambda inked along his side, and his thumb grazed over a hard, brown nipple. Colby shivered in his grasp at that, and Lachlan just kept it up, "accidentally" rubbing past it over and over, making sure to "accidentally" give the other nipple plenty of attention as well until Colby was all but leaning his full weight into Lachlan.

"Jesus, I've already been waiting a week. This is just cruel and unusual punishment." Colby jerked away from his ministrations, and simultaneously the rest of the way out of his shirt. "Turn off the lights and get naked already."

In that moment, Colby's voice had taken on an imperiousness that…well, Lachlan learned that maybe he liked being told what to do. Just a little bit. Or at least he liked it when Colby told him what to do. His cock twitched harder, and he slipped over to the light switch. He slid the dimmer down until the bulbs held only the barest of flickers, a subtle warmth that gave him just enough illumination he could see without tripping. And that he could make out the ethereal shapes of Colby as he slid out of his shoes and socks, pulled off his pants, and eventually out of his trunks altogether. Lachlan couldn't *see* the excitement he may or may not have had, but he caught outlines, shadow and highlight, and that was all that Lachlan needed to feel the heat rush through his system, the electricity crackle along his veins as he frantically followed orders. In less than a minute, he was peeling off his socks, then he crashed his mouth against that pulse point, that little hollow in Colby's neck. He had no issue finding it, as though magnetically drawn back toward it.

Colby ran his hands along Lachlan's sides, across his abs, up his back so his fingers pressed into the space between Lachlan's shoulder blades. It felt like neither of them breathed, as though they weren't scrambling together on the soft, cool sheets of the bed, as though they weren't anywhere other than with each other. Place, time, situation, it didn't matter. This was a week of pure, complete desire finally freed of its chains.

Colby bucked his hips up beneath Lachlan, pressing his hard shaft into Lachlan's thigh, and he moaned loudly. "Fuck, I feel like a teenager."

"Like you're going to just immediately blow your load?"

"Exactly." Even in the dim, Lachlan could see his smile was full, toothy. "I was hoping for a more charitable interpretation, like I was just super horny, but yeah. I don't know how long I'm going to last."

In response, Lachlan focused on his hands, heating the skin ever so slightly, and slipped his grip down, past Colby's belly button. He wrapped his fingers loosely around Colby's shaft and ever so gently stroked from the base to *almost* the head, making sure never to quite touch all those sensitive nerve endings.

"Fuuuuuuuuuck."

"You forgot to warn me you were about to swear."

Colby snorted. "I reserve the right to cuss like a sailor when you're committing war crimes against my person." He bucked his hips gently. "Dude, I'm going to—"

Lachlan locked his mouth down on Colby's as he continued stroking, going steadily faster as Colby's cock pulsed, as warmth shot forward and dripped down Lachlan's hand. When it seemed to have calmed, he pulled away, raised his hand up, and licked at the salty, musky fluid.

"I'm still...hard." Colby's speech had to slip in between panting. "Fuck me."

"You sure?"

"I didn't buy all these supplies just to get a ten second hand job." He shimmied out from underneath Lachlan, taking all his glorious body heat with him, and draped himself over the edge of the bed. "Fuck. Me."

Lachlan didn't need telling a third time. He fumbled around for the box of condoms and ripped it open, dumping the packets out on top of the bed. Then he kneeled down and spread Colby's cheeks. He couldn't see in the dark, but he pressed forward, searching with tongue and lips to locate the taut pucker that tasted just slightly of soap and slightly of sweat. He was sure he found it when Colby groaned, his muscles tightening. Lachlan stroked himself as he lapped and kissed and gently ministered to Colby's hole.

Then he pulled back. Not because he wanted to stop rimming, but because he wasn't that far behind Colby, wasn't at all sure he wouldn't jizz right then and there. He grabbed the little bottle of lube, popped the top, and dolloped it onto the tip of his middle finger. Then he went in, sliding gently inside of Colby and pressing, working the muscles apart bit by bit, diving deeper into the soft, silken interior. And he may have applied a little warmth there as well. More relaxation. Looser. More ready. It wasn't long at all before he was in to the hilt, knuckles pressing against Colby's tender skin.

"That's good." Colby's voice shot out rough and wild and, once again, authoritative. "I'm not a virgin. Go for it."

Lachlan hated to stop at all, but he had to ask. "You're sure?"

"Fuck. Me. Now."

Apparently Lachlan did need to be told again. But he had every intention of listening this time. He stood, ripped open a condom, and rolled it over his cock. Then he spread lube from the tip down and positioned himself. Slowly, he slid his hips forward, holding tight to Colby, and after a few seconds of pressure, he popped inside. "Tell me when you're okay."

Colby was breathing hard, his whole body tense for twenty seconds before he finally began to loosen up again. "All right."

And Lachlan pressed forward, letting his shaft disappear into that soft warmth as Colby's moans and whimpers filled the bedroom. Each tiny sound felt like a wave of the ocean, crashing into Lachlan as they connected together, the room filling with water. He was drowning happily in Colby, in the evening, in the warmth, in the way his hole kept contracting around Lachlan's shaft.

Finally, Lachlan was nearly all the way in. He pulled back out, and his knees shivered. That was almost enough to make him finish right there. As it was, he wouldn't last long at all anyway.

"Faster. Harder." Colby's voice was only getting more stern. "I want to feel it in the morning."

Jesus. "I though I was the one being torturous."

"I know what I want. And I want you."

A new layer of warmth settled over Lachlan at those words. He slammed back against Colby hard, enough he felt the mattress shift slightly. Back out, in, out. Skin slapped against skin. Colby's moaning turned into machine gun fire, each slam against his hips jarring the sound a little bit.

"Fuck you're tight." Lachlan had so many plans for how this would go. He could use warm hands. He could make lights dance between them. He could worship Colby's body as he laid resplendent on the bed. But this, connection, sensation, raw desire, he would take that. He would bottle it and drink it every morning if that was at all possible.

"I'm going to come."

Colby wriggled again, a clear signal he wanted free. Lachlan begrudgingly obliged, peeling off his condom as Colby lowered himself to his knees. The warmth of his mouth, the suppleness of his lips, that was all Lachlan needed to push him over the edge. He didn't even have a chance to warn Colby before his cock twitched out one, two, three, four, five, six spurts of heat, filling Colby's mouth.

All the while, Colby stoked himself, and as he pulled off and swallowed, a harsh wave rocked his body, and he finished once again, filling the air with the perfume of sex and sweat.

The seconds of silence afterward extended into eternity.

Then Colby started to laugh. Half-chuckling at first, then full, throaty peals of laughter.

"Was I that bad?"

"It was…a hundred times better…than I ever expected." He pushed himself up onto the bed and flopped backward onto it. "Can you…the lights?"

Lachlan didn't walk over, just reached out and persuaded the dimmer to slide up. As brightness returned to the space, he got the opportunity to take in every glorious centimeter of Colby's body. His chest and abdomen heaving, his legs lightly dusted with black hair, a patch of well-trimmed bush above a still half-hard cock that glistened with cum. His normally smooth, sleek hair was mussed, out of place. His glasses had been thrown aside at some point, and his normally fathomless eyes burned somewhere down in their depths.

"Thanks." Colby sighed. "I'm definitely going to feel that in the morning."

"I didn't hurt you, did I?"

"Oh, god, no." Colby sat up and slipped his glasses on. His eyes widened as he looked at Lachlan, and his gaze very obviously fell downward. "Although looking at that, I'm shocked you didn't hurt me."

"It's average, but I appreciate the flattery." That pit where Lachlan threw inconvenient thoughts roiled a little bit, but he smothered it down. *Pillow talk time, not worrying about the future time.* "How long is too long before the party guests get suspicious that you've been gone so long?"

"Soon, unfortunately." Colby rolled his shoulders back, then got up and headed for a door on the opposite side of the room. "I've got towels and stuff in here. Unless you need to keep that semen for magic."

"Oh, I wouldn't dare use semen magic on you. That's powerful shit."

"Even if I asked?"

He has no idea what he's asking. It had uses in spells. Mostly old spells, and mostly old spells to tie couples together inter-minably. "Remember, I'm a magical whore. I only cast spells for money."

The way Colby gently toweled him off was another pang. Now that they'd gone the distance, Lachlan didn't have as much ammunition at his disposal to keep the thoughts of parting at bay. Colby had changed the monotony. He'd been a bright spot on the gray, autumn coast. And he'd be heading back to college soon, amid the sun-bleached sands.

But for now, Lachlan was determined to enjoy the exhaustion in his muscles and the soft terrycloth Colby ran along his cock.

CHAPTER TEN

The next day was hard to face. The Halloween gala had gone until near midnight, although the only real standout after they got dressed and headed back down was a slightly drunken request from Harvey Christian that Lachlan show them something exciting. Apparently while they were upstairs together, word and rum had made their way around, and now basically everyone knew that Lachlan had a few tricks up his sleeve. He'd asked for high proof liquor and a feather, and with strange looks, those were provided. He poured out a small amount of the overproof rum—that was likely why everyone was so drunk on that punch—into an empty wine glass, then laid the feather on top. It was a small spell, not something that had much use, but it was one that was nice and flashy. One thing his dad had taught him how to pull off.

He ignited the feather with his fingertip, eliciting gasps, and used a little suggestion to bring the rum up into the ember-ridden feather. From there, the spell took its own effect. The initial flame lit the rum, and the nature of the spell and the will turned it into a six inch swirling vortex of fire.

After that, Lachlan got a few more requests for work, and with all *that* weighing on him, he excused himself form the party. He'd gotten a cab, leaving his car and the remainders of the bins and supplies to be retrieved in the morning. And honestly, he was happy to put that off, taking his time making much-needed coffee, grabbing a long shower, staring at his reflection in the mirror for way too long while he refused to put on clothes.

He didn't like waking up to a world where Colby wouldn't be walking into his candy shop anymore. No talking about the past, no diving deeper, no playful little flirtatious games.

But he sighed, and he got a cab again, and within fifteen minutes was in front of the Grayson house up on the cliff. Joann and Roland themselves were up on ladders taking down the lights and the butcher paper and all that from the entrance.

When he got out, Joann moved down her ladder, waving at him. "I hope you don't mind, we polished off a lot of that candy, so we just sort of packed everything up for you."

"It's your candy, so I certainly don't mind." He smiled. "Thanks for packing up. I hope you enjoyed everything."

"Enjoyed it? Of course." She chuckled. "When I stop by for that spell, I hope I can pick up a few of those piña colada lollipops? Colby told me the marshmallows probably take too long to get them done in time."

"I'll see what I can do."

"Colby's probably kicking around," said Roland, bundling up the red mesh and dropping it into a pile on the ground. "I think he wants to talk to you, anyway."

"Really?"

"Well, he was planning to call you and come to the shop," sad Joann. "My guess would be he wants to have a chat about something."

"Guess I should head inside, then. I promise I won't steal any crystal."

"And I promise we don't have any crystal at the vacation house worth stealing." And Joann was climbing back up the ladder.

Lachlan headed through the front door. This house had been cleaned exceptionally well, no sign of the previous evening's festivities aside from the single small table still filled with candy, and the plastic tubs, stacked one inside the other with the tops stacked underneath.

"Oh, good morning." Colby's voice came from the top of the stairs, and when Lachlan looked up at him, his breath caught just a bit. He was wearing a black, shimmery dressing gown, the chest open almost down to the cinching waistband. "Do you want some coffee?"

"I've already caffeinated. I just wanted to pick up my stuff."

"Oh, well let me carry it out for you. Least I can do." He headed down the stairs, and was a little slower than usual. "You definitely delivered. I feel it today."

Lachlan offered a smile, because he didn't know what he could actually say.

They headed into the ballroom, and Colby stopped, leaning against the candy table. "I kind of wanted to mention something to you today anyway, so I'm glad you came by."

"What's up?"

"I...well, it's a little weird. But I kind of like it here. I like the company." He nudged Lachlan in the side. "My parents are always on about how they'd like someone to actually stay here to watch the house. And there's a decent finance program at the University of New Hampshire I could prob-ably swap into. Since I'm changing colleges anyway."

"What?"

"I'm saying...I'm saying I'm maybe going to see you more."

"I don't want to sound super vain, but please don't move out here and leave a Berkeley education on account of how good I am in the sack."

"It would be about your personality, not your performance, and it also has nothing to do with you. UNH has been on my list for a while, now." Colby sighed. "But since we've gotten *closer*..." He shrugged. "What I'm saying is that I'll be up here. In the house. The college is only an hour away."

"That's two hours of driving every day."

"Every day I actually need to go in." He smiled. "You could be a little bit happier."

"It's a shock is all. I like the thought of seeing you more. It's just—"

"If you don't want to have to see me, you don't have to."

Shit. Lachlan immediately wrapped a hand around Colby's wrist. "It's not about that. I just want you making a happy decision for yourself, not...God, it sounds stupid, but I...we could be long distance."

"But we don't have to be." Colby grabbed his wrist back. "Look, my mom graduated from UNH. I'll be a legacy. The fact that you're here just makes the decision a lot easier." He smiled, full on and toothy. "What I really wanted to talk to you about was the house. It's big, and when I'm in class, it'll be really empty. Since you're looking for ways to cut back on your expenses."

"You want me to move in?"

"I want you to consider it." Colby brushed a hand back through his hair. "You can take time to consider it, of course. But the house will be here. I'll be here." He reached down and grabbed the stacked tubs. "Your car?"

"Right." What the hell was going on? Suddenly, Lachlan was completely off balance. So much had just happened, and not one iota of it had been what he'd expected. So it was in a slightly dumb state that he followed Colby out to the car and opened the back door for him to slide the tubs inside.

Colby grabbed him by the shoulders. "You're freaking out?"

"A little bit. I was completely expecting to not see you again after last night. I was already in the middle of freaking out and being sad. Now you're moving into my town?" Lachlan looked into those deep eyes, and a sense of calm washed over the rest of his emotions. "I'm happy. I really am. Just processing."

"You want space to process, or you want someone to talk to while you process?"

And Lachlan thought back on the feelings he kept returning to the whole night, the whole morning. *What kind of idiot doesn't take the chance to stop that kind of crap storm?* "If you have time, your mom requested some marshmallows and lollipops, so I need to get into the shop anyway."

"Well, I am an expert marshmallow cutter."

"Calm down. You're far from an expert." Lachlan smiled, and it was a little more genuine. "You do want to leave California, right? It's not me making you, but is it your family?"

"No, it's not. Like I said, I'll be a legacy. And if I'm being totally frank, the job I'm angling for after I graduate? The CEO of the company is a UNH alum, so this is another little leg up."

"Does it really make that much difference if you went to the same college as him?"

"Not always, but this guy's really proud of his college. Says it shows that you don't have to go to some huge Ivy League in order to make something of yourself." Colby nodded, then reached out and patted Lachlan's face. "I'm making my own decisions. Trust me, if I was going to be back in California, this would have been a conversation where we discussed a webcam situation. It's just fortune that we get to actually stay together instead. Take the good fortune."

Colby *had* brought a lot of good fortune into Lachlan's life in this week. He'd basically saved the business. He'd gotten

Lachlan laid. He'd been a bright spot in the drear of this coastal city. Lachlan imagined a lot of people would write that all off to a random good week, but he was a witch. When you added the right components together with the proper will, you got certain results. And everything here had come from adding Colby to his particular brew. "Well I'm happy to have you around. Maybe next time we can keep the lights on."

"Tres kinky." Colby grinned, then sighed. "I'll get dressed and head down to the shop, then?"

Lachlan closed the door of his car. "I can just drive you down. As long as you don't dawdle."

Colby backed up. "I'll be down in five."

He ran back into the house, and seemingly immediately, Joann and Roland both descended upon him, Joann speaking first. "He's really into you, I think."

"It sure looks that way."

"He asked if you could stay in the house," said Roland. "Which, for the record, as long as he's fine with it, that's fine. It's functionally going to be his place as long as he's in the area." A slow, easy smile split Roland's round face. "It'll be nice for him to not be so alone."

Beneath the combined gaze of the pair of them, given the conversation topic, Lachlan had to fight hard not to squirm. "If he wants me up here, I can be up here. If he changes his mind, I'm gone."

They both glanced to each other, contented, but luckily Colby made his reappearance before they could say anything, wearing that same black, zigzag sweater. He stopped next to Lachlan and eyed his parents. "You're not being weird, are you?"

"No weirder than usual," said Joann.

"Oh god." But Colby smiled the whole time he spoke. "Am I going to have to find a new boyfriend?"

That was a loaded word Lachlan wasn't entirely prepared

for, and he responded before he even had a chance to think. "Boyfriend?"

"Well, it's certainly in the cards, don't you think?" Colby winked at him. "As long as my parents don't scare you off."

Lachlan giggled nervously. "If my dad didn't scare you off, your parents are good." This was all a lot, and he *really* wanted to get back into the shop. Not because any of this felt wrong or bad, but just because he wanted something grounding. The depression he'd been avoiding had been yanked out from underneath him, but it still felt like nothing new had been slipped under his feet. He turned his attention to Joann. "I'm going to try to have marshmallows for you. They'd probably be ready by tonight. Lollipops, no problem."

She nodded. "We're not heading out until tomorrow, so no rush. And that little thing we discussed last night?"

"That'll be ready, too." Then he turned his focus to Colby. "Ready?"

"Of course."

❅

Lachlan made quick work of the lollipops, and was currently boiling the sugar syrup for the marshmallows. At the same time, he was whipping together a little charm bag for Joann. Tumbleweeds to make blowing away oh so easy. Nettle to make her more protected. A couple of lodestones to repel. Pretty basic stuff, and now he was sewing it up with red thread. Strength, courage, and doubly useful because these were matters of the heart.

The bells out front jingled and Lachlan set his sewing down. "I swear I locked that."

The kitchen doors came open as well, and standing there was Dorian James, looking none-too-refreshed with his hair sticking out at odd angles. He smoothed out the front of his shirt and locked his gaze onto Lachlan. "My boy."

"Breaking and entering?"

"Into my shop."

"You keep saying that, yet you don't seem to understand why you're wrong." He glanced over at Colby, trying to signal him to stay out of it this time, then rose and walked up to his father. "If you want to come into *my* shop, you need an appointment."

"I need the books."

"Sorry, that's not happening. If you could have found them, you would have by now." Lachlan pressed a finger to his father's chest, and he struck a little bit of lint hanging there alight for good measure. "I got your message, by the way. Too bad I'm not an idiot who thinks the lily and bell does anything, otherwise I might have assumed that was meant to be a threat."

"If this business closes down because you can't keep your dick where it belongs—"

Lachlan slapped him across the cheek. With his other hand, he reached up and plucked a few black hairs from his father's head. He could see the look of shock, and it wasn't from the slap. Lachlan had a part of him, now. Any witch worth a damn knew what kind of shit you could pull off with some hair, a tooth, nail clippings.

"You have no right—"

"Actually, you have no right." He reached down and lowered the heat on his sugar syrup so it wouldn't go past soft ball while he was handling this. "It's my shop. I'm gay. You're a dick. And I plan to make use of this hair to keep you at bay. What form that takes depends on how you behave right now."

"I don't care that you gay."

"That's all you've cared about since you found out." He took the little pinch of hairs and added them to a mortar and pestle, then added some salt and some of the tumbleweed spines he'd been using for Joann's charm bag. "Hot peppers to ward you off. Do I add saltpeter or rotted meat or spider carcasses to make this worse for you, or do you have something nice to say to me?"

Dorian swallowed hard. "I still want to be able to see you."

And Lachlan did believe him. Dorian was a dick, but they weren't a hateful family. Just a family with a lot of drama. So after wracking his brain for a few seconds, Lachlan added a pinch of sugar, as well as a few strands of his own hair to the mix. "When you sweeten up on me being gay, you'll find it much easier to come back, Dad." And he ground the mixture down, then blew it int his father's face.

Dorian didn't resist, which was…odd. Apparently the shock of his son reacting had done him in. Or that was the best Lachlan could figure, anyway.

"I guess I won't look at the books." Dorian brushed some of the dust from his face, then sighed. "You're only taking appointments, now?"

Lachlan glanced at Colby and smiled. "My work is worth it, and it cuts down on some of the overhead."

And Dorian smiled just a bit. "Clever."

And he walked off, that as his last word. Not without making the lights flicker on and off a few times first, though.

"He took that well," said Colby.

"Yeah. He really did." Lachlan set the mortar and pestle aside to be cleaned and checked his temp on the syrup. 237 degrees. Right in the zone. He pulled the pan off the heat and set it aside, just until the bubbles calmed down. "But that should make it harder for him to come barging into my place of business."

"And you conveniently didn't tell him that you'll be staying up on the cliff with me."

The pointed gaze, the subtle raising of Colby's tenor, the

slight shift in his posture. It wasn't merely an observation. It housed an unspoken question. *Is that happening, or no?*

"So listen. About this morning." The sugar had cooled a touch, so Lachlan turned on his stand mixer and began to pour the still steaming syrup over his gelatin. "Just so we're clear and I didn't leave you with the wrong idea: I want to spend as much time with you as is feasible. I was miserable thinking that last night was it. I just didn't want anyone making stupid decisions. You or me." He eyed Colby up and down. "Any reason you didn't mention you were moving here anyway?"

That half-controlled smile broke across Colby's face. "I may have been protecting myself a little bit. From myself. Like I said, I have a bad habit of burning fast, then fizzling. I figured if we made it all the way to the party and up to the bedroom, and we still liked each other, that was enough of a stress test to see if things would immediately crumble." He tapped his right temple. "I'm a nerd, remember? Cost-benefit analysis."

"Well, I'm just saying, I could have been a little more romantic if I knew you were sticking around."

Colby walked straight up to him. "Romantic how?"

Lachlan sighed. "A trip down to the beach at sunset. Maybe dinner and a show down at the playhouse. A nice hotel room."

"No offense, but where's that money coming from?"

"Well, I'm a witch for one." He cranked up the speed on the mixer to get some air into the marshmallows. "And for two, I have this brilliant, sexy finance major who likes me enough he wants me to move in."

"Well, those things are both true."

Lachlan leaned over and pressed his lips to Colby's. And did he make a little spark of static travel between the two of them?

Perhaps.

Want to stay up to date with Raven de Hart? Sign up for the newsletter to be notified of sales, new releases, early previews, and more!

Sign Up Here

ABOUT THE AUTHOR

Raven de Hart is the romantic alter-ego of sci-fi/fantasy author Voss Foster. Both write with a mind to diversity, inclusion, and intriguing premises, but one has more kissing and dangly bits than the other. Raven lives in a trailer in the middle of Washington State with far too many dogs, certainly more than the local law actually allows for. He is the author of many gay romance novels, with Swarm being the first of a batch of re-released books, and currently has a contemporary series (Get Baked!) and a high fantasy series (Hearts of Madijak) in the works. When not writing, he can be found in the kitchen, in the liquor cabinet, or cruising social media.

Find Raven de Hart Online
Newsletter
Facebook
Twitter
Instagram
Website